Spiral

Love & Rugby series

Susan Scott Shelley
and Chantal Mer

Shelley and Mer

Chapter One

♥

Easton

Sweat trickles down my hairline and into my eye. I swipe it away and get into line for more of our front tackle drills.

"Ball carriers, remember to turn *toward* your team. Opposition, you're not going to get a good lift if you don't have the cheek-to-ass-cheek position." Cam Davidson, the captain of the over-thirty team and owner of the company I work at, stands with his hands on his hips, breathing as hard as the rest of us.

Our under-thirty team and Cam's team practice together every week and often get together after games and outside of them.

"Cheek-to-ass-cheek?" The captain for my team, Aspen's lips curl in disgust. "Really, that's how you're explaining it?"

Cam steps closer to Aspen, and behind me Kade mumbles, "Here we go…"

The guys around us chuckle, making their own remarks about when Aspen and Cam will either kill or fuck each other. Betting on which will happen first.

Unaware of what's happening on the sidelines, Cam and Aspen stare each other down. Cam's mouth twitches like agitating Aspen is one of his favorite pastimes. "How else would you describe the hold? They need to be cheek-to-cheek to get a good take down."

Shaking his head, Aspen throws up his hands in exasperation. Ignoring Cam, he calls, "This will be the last one."

"Thank god." Kade tosses me the ball. A swath of dirt splatters his cheekbone, and grass stains both of his knees.

I catch the ball and try not to notice how cute he looks with his light brown hair matted on the side and his fair cheeks ruddy from exertion. *Try* being the operative word because there is no ignoring a man as attractive as Kade. "You're not the one who has to face one more tackle." I twist my neck to the right and then the left. The satisfying *crack crack* loosens my shoulders. "I'm gonna be sore tomorrow."

Kade grunts, but his smile shines. "Dude, you nearly knocked the wind out of me on that last hit."

The sharp chirp of the whistle sounds before I can respond, and I jog to one end of the cones as Kade heads to the other end. Another chirp, and I take off with

Kade coming at me, long legs pumping, and he's grinning. Clutching the ball, I brace for impact. Strong arms wrap around my thighs, and the heat of his face on my ass distracts me so much I almost lose my grip. His shoulder shoves into my ribs, but I twist to keep the ball out and away from my body as our momentum sends us plowing onto the grassy field. I grunt when my back hits the earth, followed by the weight of Kade on top of me. We lie there panting for two beats of my heart before he jumps off me and extends his hand, his lime-green mouthguard shining at me. The guy is always smiling like he's up to no good, but there's something incredibly appealing about it.

I clasp the offered hand, pulling myself up to standing, and chuck him the ball. "Good hit."

"I love this game." He slaps my shoulder, and we head to where our things are located.

"Mr. Easton. Mr. Easton." Olive, Cam's five-year-old daughter, runs over, her blond ponytail bouncing as she jumps over a red cone waving a piece of paper.

I stop and squat, so I'm at her level when she reaches me. Her blue eyes shine, and the freckles on her nose are more pronounced than they were at the beginning of the summer. "And what can I do for you, Miss Olive?"

As usual, she giggles when I use the prefix. Over the last three years, it's become a game of sorts with us. "I drew you a picture." She pushes the notebook paper in my face as she props herself up on my knee like it's a chair made just for her. My weak legs wobble, but I stay upright and look on as she describes the detailed scene of beakers and Bunsen burners with me and her Aunt Aileene, my boss, in white lab coats. "And over here is a rugby ball because you're going to practice after work."

"I love it. Thank you." I take the paper and neatly fold it before slipping it into the pocket of my shorts. "I'm going to hang it in the office with the other ones."

"Olive." Cam jogs over, looking worn out. "Good practice, East." He fist-bumps me, then swings Olive over his head while I switch out my cleats for sneakers. "You going to help me with the equipment?"

"But you said you'd get me a pretzel when you were done." She points to the lone food truck still on the street.

Cam's big shoulders sag, and he blows out an exhausted breath. "I will, sweetheart, but we need to clean up." He looks at me. "Our nanny left for the Peace Corps last week, and the agency hasn't found a suitable replacement. I don't know how much longer I'll last without help."

"You two get your pretzels. I'll grab the equipment and meet you at your car." I give him a slight shove toward the food truck and jog off.

"Thanks," Cam calls.

I wave and pick up one of the dozens of cones sprinkling the field. Cam is one of those guys you'd do anything for, not only because he'd do the same for anyone, but because he's just an all-around nice guy and great dad. I've never seen a parent as involved and dedicated as Cam.

"Need help?" Kade grabs the green cone I was reaching for, teeth shining bright.

Here's the thing, if I weren't dating the hottie weather guy, Storm Breen, from Channel 6, I'd be interested in seeing if things with Kade would... go somewhere. And before you ask, yes, that is Storm's actual name. He has two sisters named Windy and Misty and a brother named Dusty. What were their parents thinking?

But back to Kade... He has this internal glow that draws anyone in his vicinity to him, me included. He's adventurous, unconstrained, and easygoing. Essentially, the complete opposite of me in almost every way.

"Help would be nice." I bump his hip with mine, enjoying the contact more than I should considering I'm in a relationship.

"First one to collect the most cones, wins." He darts across the field with more energy than one should have after an hour-long rugby practice in the middle of the week.

I scoop up the cone closest to me. "Wins what?"

He turns and raises his arms out from his sides as he jogs backward. "Bragging rights."

"You're on." I bolt toward the line of cones in the middle of the pitch as droplets of rain begin their descent. The roar of Kade's laughter echoes across the field as he rushes me, taking me down in a side-on tackle like we practiced earlier in the evening. Cones fly from my grasp and into the air as we slide across the grass that is quickly becoming wetter with each passing minute. Kade hops to his feet, collecting the scattered cones. "Not fair." Swiftly, I haul myself to standing, but the field is devoid of all equipment.

Kade holds up the red and green plastic turrets, the tease of his smirk making it hard to do anything other than grin. "Looks like I'm the winner."

"If you need to cheat for bragging rights, so be it." I push his shoulder before grabbing the equipment bag and holding it open.

Kade drops his stolen stash into the netted sac as the rain picks up. "Man, I'm gonna give Storm shit. He told me the rain was supposed to hold off until ten."

"Storm Breen?" I cinch the bag closed while Kade grabs our water bottles and backpacks. "I didn't know you two knew each other."

"The one and only. We've been dating for a few weeks. His schedule is a little tough, but we've been managing."

I freeze, my limbs no longer registering the messages firing from my synapses. "Pardon me?"

Looking with curiosity, Kade cocks his head to the side. "You okay?" His hand on my forearm singes. "You look a little queasy."

Water pelts my cheeks with tiny torpedoes of sting in coordination with the pricking at my insides. "Did you say you're dating Storm Breen?"

"Ye-es." The word is elongated in a way that makes it sound like he's unsure.

"Meteorologist, Storm Breen? *Wake up with Storm*, from Channel 6, Storm Breen?" My stomach calcifies into hundreds of malignant tumors as blood drains from my face.

Hyper-focused, Kade's eyes dart between mine, and he leans in closer, inspecting me. "Seriously, Easton, you're starting to freak me out. You look like you're gonna puke." He presses the back of his hand to my forehead. "Are you coming down with the flu or something?"

I swat his hand away while bitterness simmers on the verge of boiling over to rage. "Answer the question."

"Yeah, I've been dating Storm for about three weeks." His eyes are round with what looks like worry. "If you want, I'm sure I could get you an autograph or something."

I throw my head back, my laughter more scoff than jocular, and stomp to Cam's vehicle. "I can't fucking believe it." A hurricane of thrashing thoughts, or more precisely, thoughts of thrashing one lying, sack-of-shit meteorologist, threaten to submerge my lifeboat-sized relationship. "I've worked around that jerk's schedule for three fucking months."

Was he out with someone else every time he told me he had to get to bed early? I hadn't questioned the reasoning since he had to be on the air at four-thirty every morning.

Just as I reach Cam's car, hands on my shoulders spin me around. Gone is the ever-present smile, in its place, the disheartened curve of usually playful lips and two deep crevices between his brows. "What did you say?"

"I," I jab my finger into my sternum, "have been dating that no-good piece of shit for the last three months." Rage at Storm flogs me as disappointment of another relationship failure punctures the little remaining hope I had of finding a good man.

Kade's eyes bug, and his mouth goes slack before his jaw clenches and ticks. "So let me get this straight... The guy you've been dating for the last three months is the same guy who told me he hasn't been in a serious relationship in two years?"

"He said that?" I thump my fist against my thigh, my voice laced with edgy control. *"He's* the one who pursued *me*." My pulse roars with the volume of my voice.

Wind swirls angry blobs of water until they are coming at us sideways. With Olive in his arms, Cam races to the car, the *beep* indicates he's unlocked the car before he reaches us. Working off adrenaline, embarrassment, and hurt, I open the back of Cam's SUV and hurl the equipment bag in just as he and Olive reach us. "Thanks, guys." He slips

Olive into the back seat and helps her with her buckle. "See you Saturday."

Kade and I wave and watch as scarlet tail lights disappear in a sea of red. Neither of us says anything as our rain-soaked clothes stick to our skin. I can't believe I fell for another cheating asshole. And after being so careful... not jumping into anything... Yet here I am again. Clutching the hem of my wet shirt, I use it to wipe my dripping face and wish it was as easy to wipe away my stupidity. How many times will it take before I stop falling for smooth-talking liars?

"This is bullshit." Kade tugs on my arm. "Let's go."

"Go where?"

Fingers still wrapped around my wrist, Kade leads me to a motorcycle. "We're going to confront Storm."

"Now?" Without thought, I take the helmet he hands me from under the seat. "But he'll be asleep."

"So..."

"So, he has to be up early."

This time, when Kade flashes his smile it's with a hint of cynicism. "All the more reason to do it now." He straps on his helmet and shifts his backpack from his back to his front. "That dickwad doesn't deserve to get one ounce of beauty rest after what he did to you. That he did it to you with *me* only makes me want to pluck out each follicle of hair on his body with tweezers." He takes the helmet from my hands and plops it onto my head, then adjusts the strap.

"We're going as a united front. There's no way he's snaking his way out of this." Swinging a leg over the bike, he pats the seat behind him. "Get on."

"Maybe we should think about this first." Even my anger and outrage can't change the scientist I am. And right now, based on my qualitative observations, I'm in the midst of formulating a hypothesis on the best way to neuter a meteorologist.

"Why?"

I shrug. "At least, let's change."

"Nope." The bike comes to life with a rumble. "Get on, East. We're doing this, and we're doing it now. There's nothing to think about."

Reluctantly, I do as he says. "I've never been on a motor-cycle before."

He wraps my arms around his midsection until my front is pressed to his back. Being this close to him without a rugby ball in one of our hands catapults a thrill along my spine. "Hold on and move with me." With a reassuring pat, he flips down the face shield. "I'll keep you safe."

My stomach lurches into my throat when he pulls out into traffic, and I pin my knees tightly to him while squeez-ing his middle. He's warm and solid and self-possessed. And there's a whisper deep inside me that says Kade would keep me safe on more than just his bike.

Chapter Two

Kade

As I maneuver through the rainy streets of the city I've come to love and call home for the last three years, the feel of Easton's arms banding around me and his front plastered against my back is arousing as hell. And I don't have to feel guilty about it since we're en route to dump our cheating, lying boyfriend's ass.

Aware that Easton's not used to the bike, I take each turn carefully. The first time I saw him, at a crowded meet and greet before my first rugby game last fall, I was struck by his gorgeous dark brown eyes and drawn in by the sculpted angles and planes of his face and how his thick black hair flopped over his forehead like it begged to be brushed aside by a lover's hand. Tall, tanned, and athletic from the first glance, I've learned over the past three rugby seasons that he's also exceedingly kind.

He deserves way better than what Storm did to him.

When we reach Storm's building, my pulse ticks up the way it does when I'm lining up on the rugby field, ready to engage with the enemy. Storm's Jaguar gleams in can't-miss-me red. I pull into the spot beside it and kill the engine. As I remove my helmet, Easton's arms slide from the tight grip he had around my torso, but when his fingers reach the sides of my waist, he stops moving. The pressure of those ten points of contact is both reassuring and makes me want to do whatever I can to keep him safe. Turning my head, I lock eyes with him. We're close enough to kiss. My lips tingle at the thought. "Ready?"

"Yeah." His fingers tighten on my waist before he disentangles himself and swings off the bike. Missing the absence of his body, I follow.

After stowing the helmets, I lead the way toward the building's front door. Holding a finger against Easton's lips, I press the button on the intercom for Storm's apartment. "Let me do the talking for now."

He nods, and I slide my finger away. My pulse jumps at the way Easton's tongue swipes over his lips as though he's trying to soak up the flavor of my touch. But maybe that's just wishful thinking on my part.

The softness of Easton's lips, the vulnerability in his dark gaze, the way he's watching me, all of it compounds into a desire to kiss him and protect him. I press the button again, holding it down. The incessant buzzing noise echoing through the apartment will drive Storm from his bed.

Crackling comes through the speaker, followed by Storm's voice. "Yes?"

"Hey, it's me. Thought I'd stop by to surprise you."

"Kade?"

I quirk a brow at Easton. "Would you be expecting anyone else?"

"Uh, no. Of course not. But I didn't think I'd see you tonight. Now's not a good time."

No way are we waiting to confront him. Shaking my head at Easton, I pour sweetness into my voice. "I'll only stay a minute. Please?"

"I, I guess. Okay. Come on up."

With a soft buzz, the lock on the door releases. Yanking it open, I motion for Easton to enter, then follow him through. We're soaked. Our practice jerseys and shorts are plastered to our skin. We're leaving wet sneaker prints on the polished lobby floor. Easton's hair, which had been flattened by the combination of the helmet and the rain, is spiked from his hands running through the thick strands.

He taps the button for the elevator and I can't stop myself from laying my hand on his shoulder. "You okay?"

"Sure." But his tight expression and the anger, shock, and hurt rolling off of him suggests otherwise. He dated Storm for three months, a hell of a lot longer than my three weeks. Of course, he'd feel the shock and hurt deeper. Plus, in addition to being kind, Easton is super considerate, steady and loyal. He'd never do to anyone what Storm has done to us. Nor would I. The desire to protect him is back, rearing up like a lion ready to defend its mate.

I tighten my hold, squeeze twice in sympathy, then let go. "Liar. But it's okay, and I understand."

The elevator opens with a low ping. Easton takes a deep breath. "Ready?"

"Let's hit Storm with a hurricane." I usher us both into the car.

One corner of his lips raises in a half-smile as he presses the button for Storm's floor. "Hit him with a hurricane?"

"I know, lame, but it's the best weather-related joke I can think of right now." My stomach tightens as we rise higher. I don't know what I'll say when face-to-face with Storm, but if he says anything at all to hurt Easton further… I don't know what I'll do about that either, but it won't be pretty or nice.

Gaze trained on the electronic numbers flashing with each floor, Easton rocks back on his heels. "So how are we going to play this?"

The car comes to a stop and the doors open. I grab his hand. "Beats me. Let's find out."

As we pad over the lush carpet, I keep his warm hand curled around mine, drawing support and giving it. When we reach Storm's door, I gently nudge Easton away from the view should Storm glance out his peephole, then knock.

The door opens just wide enough to show Storm's face. He smiles at me and the urge to plow my fist into his lying mug is so strong, only the feel of Easton's hand on my arm reins me in. The door handle jostles like Storm is clinging to it, but he doesn't open the door any wider. "Hi, Kade."

"Can I come in?"

A thud followed by footsteps comes from inside the apartment and Storm's blue eyes dart guiltily as he turns his head. He's not alone. I shove my sneaker into the space between the door and the frame so he can't close me out.

An interior door closes. Definitely not alone. He whips his gaze back to me. "So..."

"You have company?" Pressing my hand on the door, I brace my muscles.

Smile strained at the edges, Storm shakes his head. "It's not what it looks like."

"No? I bet it's *exactly* what it looks like." I shove the door, forcing it open wider. Storm jumps back, gaze darting from me to the bedroom door. Free from his hold, the front door swings inward. I kick it the rest of the way open, and step inside. Easton's hand finds mine and fingers curled tight, he joins me. Shoulder to shoulder. Hand in hand. A united front.

Storm's mouth gapes open, his eyes are rounded wide as his focus flashes between Easton and me. "What? How?"

"Exactly." I focus all of my hurt and betrayal into that one word. "What did you think you were doing, screwing around with the two of us, and how did you think you'd get away with it?"

Holding his hands up, Storm backs away a few steps. "Can you blame me? You're both gorgeous."

"We were supposed to be exclusive." Easton's words are quiet, banked fury. "You cheating, lying bastard."

"Yeah," I jump in. "How is it that you've been dating Easton for three months, yet told me three weeks ago that you weren't exclusive with anyone?"

Storm flicks an imaginary piece of lint off his shirt. "Words mean different things to different people. Not my fault Easton took serious to mean exclusive."

Shock at his statement leaves me speechless, but the chaser of anger ignites an explosion of indignation. I drop East's hand so I can lunge at the misguided meteorologist unencumbered and avenge the hurt his words and actions have caused Easton. "Are you *kidding* me? You..."

Storm retreats farther, falling onto his couch— the same couch where I sat last Saturday night—and holds up a throw pillow like a shield.

Hands clamp onto my shoulders, holding me back. Easton's breath feathers over my neck, warm and soft and close. "Don't, Kade. He's not worth it."

The bedroom door opens and a guy who looks to be about our ages, mid-to-late twenties, stands in the doorway, shirt half-unbuttoned, a frown darkening his face. "Storm, what's going on? You told me this would only take a second."

Leaning into Easton, I fire a pointed look at Storm. *Another* guy. I wonder how many others there are. "Sorry, man. Storm is busy explaining why he thought he could get away with cheating on us both."

"Cheating?" The guy comes into the room, gaze roaming from Storm to Easton to me, then back to Storm. "Not cool, dude. I think I'd better go."

"No, wait." Storm jumps from the couch and rounds it, giving Easton and me a wide berth as the guy makes his escape. "Look, guys, I'm sorry. I..." He drags his hands through his hair, ruining his carefully styled blond locks. "I'm not ready to be more settled. I wanted to be with you—all of you—so I said what I thought you'd want to hear to make you happy."

His confused logic leaves me shaking my head as I try to untangle the words and intentions.

"Lying to us isn't the way to make anyone happy." The words snap from Easton. Pressed against my back, his muscles vibrate with tension. I don't think he realizes that his hands are digging into my shoulders. "If you'd been upfront..."

"Yeah, right." Storm laughs, but the sound is frustrated and bitter. "I've tried being open about what I... Let's just say it doesn't often get me many repeat dates with the same guy."

Silence hangs heavy in the air. The dejected, defeated slump of Storm's shoulders almost makes me feel sympathy, empathy, for him. Almost. If it hadn't been for the hurt he's caused Easton. Easton's hands slip from my shoulders. I know him, know how kind he is, know that even in this moment, in spite of that hurt, in light of Storm's revelation, he's probably feeling sympathy for him too.

I step back until we're standing side by side once more and wrap my arm around Easton's shoulders. "Well, you need to think of something better, Storm. Because those lies just cost you this guy right here. He's special."

Easton's eyes widen. He holds my gaze for a beat and an emotion I can't name flickers across his face. His hand grazes across my back as he looks at Storm. "And you lost Kade too. I don't put up with lies or cheating. Neither does he."

Wringing his hands, Storm takes a step toward us. "Guys—"

"No. No more words. We're done." Easton holds up a hand to cut him off. "Come on, Kade. Let's go."

I tamp down on my desire to high-five Easton for holding his ground and follow him from the condo, not bothering to close the door behind us. We're quiet as we walk down the hall. Once we're on the elevator, Easton closes his eyes and drops his head back. "I can't believe we did that."

"Felt good, didn't it?" I brace my legs as the car lurches down. Looking at Easton, I feel more unsteady than I should. "Let's get a drink to celebrate."

"A drink?"

"Why not?" We exit the car and our sneakers squeak as we cross the lobby. "The rain has let up. Let's raise a glass to the end of the storm."

"In more ways than one." Easton draws in a breath then nods. "Okay. I'm in."

"Great."

Twenty minutes later, we're tucked into the corner of a crowded pub, beers in hand, discussing Storm.

"Who knows how many people he's with?" Shaking his head, Easton lifts a glass of amber ale to his lips. "I'm just happy he and I hadn't stopped using condoms."

I nod, filled with a mixture of gratitude and relief that the more minutes that go by, the more Easton is returning to his happy self. "Right? Same here. Where did you meet him?"

"Alter Ego. The night they did their annual celebrity bartender charity fundraiser." Easton pushes his hair off his forehead and my fingers itch to help him do it. The queer-owned nightclub is a welcoming space and with our rugby buddy Mateo working there as a bouncer, our team-mates spend at least one weekend a month at the club.

I take another pull of my beer. I'd missed that event because I'd been stuck at work. "I met him there too, last month, when we visited Mateo. Storm came in with one of the morning news anchors about an hour after you left."

"Oh." His lips thin. "Well, I'm sorry I didn't stick around."

"Me too." My words are heavy with longing. Maybe things lined up the way they did today for a reason. Maybe it's time to test the waters. "If we're being honest, instead of him, I'd have preferred dancing with you."

Easton gapes at me. His glass lands on the table with a loud smack. "Me?"

"Of course. Like you don't know how gorgeous you are." Nerves edge my stomach, my heartbeat quickens, and all I can do is hold tight to my beer and hope Easton reciprocates my feelings. "Since we're both single now, I can say it. You're stunning. I've thought so since the first time I saw you."

He dips his head and the shy smile only makes him more adorable. "Neither of us was unattached back then."

"No. Not then." But now...

His gaze searches mine, and my muscles tighten, drawing my spine up straight. Squaring my shoulders, wondering if I measure up to his scrutiny, I hold his gaze, hoping he finds what he needs. His teeth scrape over his lower lip.

"My last ex was a cheater too. I'd really thought Storm was different."

I read the unspoken words, that he hopes future prospects will also be different. Maybe even seeking reassurance that *I'll* be different. "So did I. He talked a good game, didn't he?" Annoyance and disappointment over Storm's actions is all I feel about the short-lived relationship. We weren't together long enough for deeper emotions to emerge. "I hope he finds what he's looking for."

"I do too. I hope we all do. Let's not waste any more time talking about him."

I nod. "Agreed. What are you looking for?"

The tips of his ears grow red as he studies his beer. "Honesty. Loyalty. Love."

Those three simple words strike an empty place deep inside me. I want them too. So much of my life has been cycles of upheaval, mostly created by my own actions. Longing to find the place where I belong, the people I belong with, and the ones who belong to me, I've kept moving. Philly has been the only place that's called for me to settle in. The connections I feel with the guys on the team, the guys at work, and the guy across the table from me make staying appealing in ways I've never felt before. "I want them too."

At my words, Easton jerks his focus from the beer. We watch each other and with his nervous smile and widened eyes, he looks as raw and vulnerable and open as I feel.

What we're sharing here is deeper than words, it's like secrets from our souls.

His hands flex, open then closed before his shoulders droop like they're carrying the weight of the world and his expression shifts to a weariness that tugs on my heart and makes him seem much older than his twenty-seven years. "Sometimes, I think... maybe it's all just too much work, you know? The dating, the opening up, the risking, and then the pain and heartache."

I do know. It can be exhausting and frustrating. But also exhilarating and rewarding. "The road to love is a wild ride."

Easton stares at me for a long moment. "That was almost poetic."

Slightly embarrassed, I smile and shrug. "It's also something I read on an advertisement for a motorcycle."

We both laugh and the space between us is filled with warmth and light. Everything with him is easy and effortless. And I want more.

"I guess you'd see a lot of motorcycle ads where you work." Easton leans across the table, pitching his voice louder as the crowd around us cheers at a ballgame on TV. "You've been at the repair shop almost a year now, haven't you? I remember you started there right after you joined the rugby team."

Blinking at him, I nearly choke on the mouthful of beer. He remembers that? "I can't believe it's been almost a year.

Feels like you and the guys have been a part of my life for longer than that. You know, back then, I had a chance to take a job in Vegas with one of my old buddies, but something told me to stay here. And then I met you all."

Easton's leg brushes mine under the table. "I'm happy you stayed. I know you moved around a lot before. How many times has it been in total? You told me at one of our happy hours early on, but I can't remember."

"I moved twelve times when I was growing up. And I guess that kind of stayed with me because I moved four more times after turning eighteen. Being in Philly for the last three years is the most permanent I've been in a long time." Two years at a living space, city, or job has been my average. I get restless.

"I'm the opposite. Born and raised here. Went to college here too." Easton lowers his gaze to the tabletop. "I guess that seems boring."

"You could never be boring, East. You're a scientist, which I think is sexy as hell. You work on developing products for a condom company that's gaining tons of attention for sustainability, which is admirable and important. You do volunteer work to save the planet, also admirable and important. And you play a sexy sport in your spare time."

His rueful smile pulls at me. "You play the same sport, Kade."

I shrug and slowly drag the edge of my sneaker along his instep. "Seems sexier when I think about you playing it."

He ducks his head again. That shy smile is back and so is the hair flopping over his forehead. He looks disheveled and utterly kissable. "Are you…"

"Flirting? I'm trying."

His brown gaze turns serious and meets mine, holding it as his tongue swipes over his lips and he draws his bottom lip between his teeth. "I don't know what to say."

The last thing I'd want to do is make him uncomfortable. "If it's *stop*, I will."

As we watch each other, a smile forms like the first rays of morning light and grows to beaming and beautiful. "It's not stop."

"Good." Setting my beer aside, I lay my hand atop his on the table. Nerves jump and writhe at the feel of his touch, and at the knowledge that he's into me too, and into this whatever-it-is between us. But where do we go from here? I can think of several options, but Easton needs to set the pace, especially in light of everything that's happened tonight.

As if he's reading my mind, he says, "Tonight's been a whirlwind."

"It has." Trailing my fingers over the back of his hand and fingers, I soak up his warmth, then sit back to allow him space and show that I'm not going to push him. "Let's finish our beers. I'll give you a lift home."

"It's okay. I don't live that far, I can walk."

I calculate the distance. He's at least ten blocks from here. "No way. It's getting late and still raining. I'll take you."

He holds me tight as we ride through the streets. Flashes of lightning and rumbles of thunder provide a soundtrack to the evening. Easton shifts closer to me with each one. I don't love riding my bike in the rain, and I really don't like being out in a thunderstorm.

When we get to Easton's building, he directs me into the covered garage. "You can park in my spot. I don't use it."

He doesn't own a car, and gets around by bicycle or on foot. Mr. Sustainability, through and through. If he wants me to park, does that mean he wants me to come in?

Once we're in his spot, he climbs off the bike and removes the helmet. "Come up and wait out the storm. I don't want to worry about you getting struck by lightning while you're driving home."

"You sure it's okay?"

He hands me the helmet. "I wouldn't have invited you in otherwise."

"Okay, then." I get off the bike and stow the helmets. Walking side by side with him through his building gives me a flashback to walking through Storm's building together and the surge of protectiveness I felt then. It lingers now, under the currents of interest and the desire to hold

Easton tight and kiss him until we both forget anything exists except each other.

His apartment is decorated in shades of green, blue, and gray, with leather furniture and artful pieces like it was put together by a professional decorator. A far cry from my spartan studio apartment.

Easton drops the bag with his rugby gear by the door, then takes mine from me and sets it down. He kicks off his sneakers, gesturing for me to do the same. "Make yourself comfortable."

After setting my sneakers in a neat line next to my bag, I follow him into the kitchen. The decorator's touch continues and I spy glimpses of organization, labels and containers, and rows of spices in alphabetical order. His place is lived-in, homey, and established. At twenty-six, I'm only a year younger than Easton, but he seems leaps and bounds ahead of me in the I-have-my-life-together department.

He hands me a bottle of water from his equally organized fridge. On the way back to the living room, I get a glimpse into his bedroom. More grays and greens, and matching furniture. My space will never measure up.

We settle together on the couch. Easton taps his bottle of water against mine. "Tonight was... unique. I'm happy we went through it together."

Holding his gaze, I swallow a sip. "Me too. We make a good team."

"Thanks for spurring me into taking action." He lays his hand on my thigh. Warm and firm, the touch burns into my skin.

He's beautiful by lamplight, against the backdrop of the storm raging outside and raindrops battering the windows. I set my water aside as lightning cracks across the sky. The boom of thunder follows.

When I turn back, Easton has shifted much closer. His gaze meets mine and he leans in, focus dropping to my mouth. My lips tingle and my blood throbs with the desire to kiss him. I slide my hand over his chest, over the damp jersey material, and rest my fingers along the soft skin of his chin and neck. I've fantasized about this moment so many times and it's actually happening. Me, kissing Easton. Wow. My heartbeat hammers as we come together.

Our lips touch, all heat and softness. Easton tastes like beer and raindrops, fresh and cool like autumn evenings.

The sound he makes, part pleased murmur and part groan, vibrates into me. It's like thunder and lightning. Quaking and deep, flashing and electric. His hand fists the front of my shirt and he drags me closer, angling his head for a deeper kiss. I open for his tongue, teasing it with mine. Want and need spiral together, a tempest raging through my body.

Easton's soft moan goes straight to my cock. I give into the urge to roam his torso, skating my touch under his shirt, taking my time learning the ridges and dips of his muscles and to appreciate the softness of his skin and the way he leans into my touch. Pushing his hair off his forehead, I slide my fingers through silky strands the way I've dreamed of doing for far too long. His touch rakes over my skin, hot and possessive, making my knees weak, my cock hard, and my heart yearn for more. Our kisses go on and on while gasps and quiet words guide our explorations.

We rid each other of our practice jerseys. Easton journeys his gaze over my arms and chest like he's cataloging every inch. Then his hands follow, tracing and seducing, making me quiver and writhe. I do the same, hungry to see and touch and explore even more without the barrier of material.

Interlocking symbols on his left pec give a nod to his Taiwanese, Mexican, Spanish, and Irish heritage. I've seen the tattoo several times when he's pulled off his jersey at the end of rugby games, and I've always been curious about exploring it up close and personal. I run my fingertip over the lines of ink, tracing the characters for bravery and wisdom, the pink dahlia, the red carnation, and the green shamrock.

Diving back into kissing like it's another form of breathing, we stretch out on his couch. The full length of him lined up against my body, the heat and softness of his skin, the clever play of his fingers teasing out my sensitive spots, and the intimacy this position provides—all of it feels amazing.

Thunder and lightning continue to crack and boom and the lights flicker, but stay on. A particularly loud clap of thunder breaks, echoing like an explosion is occurring directly over the building. I startle, grabbing onto Easton and he jolts, arms banding around me so tight breath is locked in my lungs and his fingers tug in my hair.

"Sorry, didn't mean to grab so tight," I murmur. Lightening my hold, I range kisses along his jaw.

"It's fine." He takes a shaky breath and holds my gaze and for a moment, I think he's going to say something further, but then he angles his head and presses his lips to mine.

His kiss is like its own hurricane, wrecking me for anyone else. His touch is the same. With him, I'm barreling into something big, something that makes every cell in my body yearn. He is the cause and the cure.

We're both hard and rocking our hips together. Laying half on him, I palm his cock through his shorts, squeezing his thickness. My cock throbs and jumps in response to his touch and to thoughts of my hands bringing him pleasure. He thrusts his hips up and clamps his hands onto my waist. "Kade. Kade."

My name in that breathless whisper brings me to the edge. Grinding my cock into his hip, I increase the stroking rhythm. He stops me only to edge down his shorts, eliminating one of the barriers. Kissing him, I continue to play, to tease, guided by his gasps and groans. The wet patch on his tented boxers grows bigger. We both tug the material away. Once his cock is freed, I grasp him properly, stroking and squeezing and laving attention on every inch. The sight of my hand wrapped around him and him stretched out beside me is almost enough to make me lose control. "You feel good, East. So good."

"Kade. I'm so close." The admission is as intimate, soft, and sexy as his gaze holding mine in this moment. His hips lock and his back arches. I keep working my thumb over the sensitive head and pumping the shaft. His lips part, eyes close, and strong fingers dig into my skin. A series of low groans fill the air between us as his cock pulses its release.

Determined to draw out every bit of pleasure, I keep jacking him, slower, through the smaller quakes, through his arching into my touch, until he lays his hand atop mine with a lazy smile. I gaze down at him and the rumpled shorts at his thighs, the messy hair, the blissed-out expression. "You look so sexy."

"Your turn now." He tugs my shorts and boxers down to mid-thigh, kicks free of his own clothing, and then urges me until I'm laying on top of him. I groan when my bare cock touches the hot skin and taut muscles of his stomach and the slippery spend of his release. His hands at my waist encourage me to rock against him. "Come for me, Kade. Come on me."

Elbows propped on either side of his shoulders, laying between his legs, I gaze at him as I move. Our position isn't lost on me. I roll my hips into his body, picturing myself thrusting deep inside him. Like he's picturing that too, he wraps his legs around my waist, heels digging into my ass to keep me close to him.

Eyes heavy-lidded with desire enrapture me. I want this and so much more with him. The sensations storming through me send me closer and closer, and I increase the pace, chasing the pleasure. He leans up and nips my lower lip. The playful bite catches me on a delicious thrust and I lose control. My orgasm hits like a tidal wave. Hips jerking recklessly, I ride the crest as Easton's whispered words and strokes and kisses carry me all the way through.

Panting, I collapse onto him. His arms wrap around my torso, welcoming me to stay, and while I'm too boneless to move, his lips are within easy reach, and they curve into a smile before closing over mine.

The rain continues to pelt the windows. We lay together for long moments, holding each other, listening to the patter of drops tapping the glass. Easton is warm and cuddling me and I can't believe I'm really here, in his apartment, wrapped around him, and that we've just shared orgasms.

His lips trail over my cheek, lingering on my mouth. Kissing him is addicting. "Come on, let's shower. I'll lend you some clothes."

Movements hampered by the waistbands of my boxers and shorts constricting my thighs, I stand. Offering him a hand, I pull him up. As I tug up my clothes and he uses his shirt to wipe our combined releases from his stomach, I glance out the window. The lightning has stopped. "The storm seems to be letting up."

His gaze shoots to mine and he stops fussing with his shorts, leaving them riding low on his hips. In two steps, he eliminates the distance between us. Easton slides his arms around my waist and touches his lips to mine. "It's still raining. Stay over."

Falling into his kiss and wrapping him in my arms, I nod. I don't want to leave, and thankfully, I don't have to.

Holding my hand, he leads the way down the hall. When he flashes a smile at me over his shoulder, it's intimate and sexy and I'm filled with a sharp longing to have him in my life in a significant way.

He turns on the spray. As we shed our shorts and boxers, a new worry twists like a thorny vine through my chest. What if Easton decides that tonight should be a one-time thing? If he wakes up in the morning with regrets? Or, if we are on the precipice of something new, so soon after things with Storm ended, that makes me his rebound relationship. Those rarely last. I don't want to lose him because of timing.

Gripping the edge of the sink, I don't know the best way to articulate any of that. "Easton..."

"Yeah?" He sticks his hand into the water and grins at me. "The temperature is perfect. You ready?"

Looking at him, those dark brown eyes, his gentle spirit, I can't walk away. If tonight is all we'll have, then I'm going to soak up every

single second. "Let's dive in."

Under the hot spray, we wrap our arms around each other and our lips meet once more. Kissing him and holding him is more of a thrill than any motorcycle ride. I don't know where this will lead, but I'll take whatever Easton will give me.

Chapter Three

♥

Easton

RAIN BATTERS THE WINDOW like a thief attempting to break in, stealing me from my sleep. In the distance, a rumble of thunder reverberates. Darkness envelops the room creating a cocoon of security from the storm. But it's the solid leg draped over mine and the soft snoring coming from the pillow beside me that soothes and steadies.

Ever since being caught in a thunderstorm while camping when I was eight, storms make me more than a little nervous. I suppose being startled awake by the crack of a giant oak tree being struck by lightning and falling into the middle of one's campsite will do that. But last night, with Kade, the storm was more of a distant drizzle than a pounding squall, and for once, I didn't panic with every taunting thump of thunder.

Lying on his back, Kade's mouth hangs loose, and his wavy hair flops over his forehead. His handsome face is relaxed, and he looks even more tranquil than he does when he's awake. I trace my fingers over the top of his muscled thigh to assure myself he's really here and luxuriate in the feel of the hair poking my fingertips. At the boom of thunder—louder, closer—followed by a flash of lightning, I jolt and count as I exhale, my fingers digging into Kade's skin.

"Hey." The groggy, raspy word sends a shot of electricity surging through me. Turning to his side, he uses the leg draped over me to pull me closer. Arm around my middle, nose burrowed in the crook of my neck, hot breath on my skin, he says, "What's wrong?"

I almost shared my fear with him last night, but telling the guy you've fantasized about that you're afraid of thunderstorms is not something most men in their late twenties are eager to do. I'd like to say I'm the exception, but I'm not. "Can't sleep." Glancing at the clock, I trail a finger along his spine. "It's after two. Go back to sleep or you'll be exhausted tomorrow."

Another clap followed by a flash, and I tense.

Warm lips press my jaw. "You don't like the storm?"

"I'm not a fan, no." Leaning into him, I concentrate on the tingle his touch elicits.

Holding me tighter, he rubs his stiff shaft against my hip, immediately calling forth my erection like some kind of pied piper of penises. His teeth graze the sensitive skin above my collarbone, and a dribble of pre-cum wets the sheet covering our naked bodies. The rain strengthens, intensifying with the roar of the wind. There's an ear-splitting crash, followed immediately by the room lighting up, but before I can bolt from the bed, Kade is over me, hand wrapped around my cock, mouth pressed to mine. Pushing me into the mattress, the weight of his body grounds me as his tongue seeks entrance. Cloaking my arms around his shoulders, I clutch him to me just in case he decides to leave.

"I'm here," he murmurs against my lips. Then he shifts until I can feel more than see him peering at me. "I'm not going anywhere unless you want me to, East."

The gentle swipe of fingers across my forehead as he brushes away an errant piece of hair mixed with the sweet determination of his words, causes my throat to constrict. I shake my head and hope he can feel it because forming words is impossible right now. I don't want him to go. Ever.

"Good." With a gentle thrust, the silky steel of his cock brushes against mine. My eyes nearly roll back in my head. He feels so damn good. When he wraps his hand around both our dicks, I want to weep with joy. His moan nourishes even as it slaughters. "You're perfect."

Savoring this time, this man, I shove all thoughts that this is a rebound thing for both of us far, far away. For a year, I've wondered what it would be like to be with Kade, and for a year, I've stepped aside when others have expressed interest. But now, I'm taking what I want, and I'll deal with the consequences tomorrow. Kissing him, I lick and taste lips that mold to my mouth like they were made specifically for me. From the tickle of his close-cropped beard to his plump lower lip, begging to be tugged between my teeth, it was all designed for me. *He* was designed for me.

The thought jostles me but Kade rolls us to our sides, disintegrating all notions as he strokes and squeezes our shafts. Running the pad of his thumb over my slick slit, he trails soft kisses along my jaw, neck, and clavicle. Skin on fire, breathing sporadic, the contrast of his soft lips with the firm clutch on our dicks, my senses are overloaded.

"More," I beg, gripping his ass and throwing my leg over his. The power of his body under my fingertips begs to be explored and revered. "I need more."

He presses his forehead to mine, his chest rises and falls, and the heat of his breath caresses my lips. "Tell me what you need."

"You." The single word comes out throaty and breathless, and at Kade's sudden stillness, I want to haul it back in. Instead, I increase the pressure of my leg around him, hooking him to me, ready to blame exhaustion and the exhilaration of his touch on my lack of filter.

Releasing our dicks, he brings his hands to my face, strumming his thumbs along my cheeks. "You have me."

Before I can fully process what he's said and what it means, I'm on my back, and the mouth that was made for me is skimming a path along my torso. The tease of his tongue laps the moisture from the tip of my cock. Entwining my fingers in the tangle of his waves, I jut my hips up for more. He rolls my balls in his hand and flattens his tongue, licking my straining shaft from base to tip. A throbbing tingle skyrockets up my spine, hitting every vertebra. But when he swallows me in one swift move, the tingle quakes and launches back down in screaming glory to my dick.

With every suck, every tease, every nip, incoherent nonsense falls from my lips. I yank at his hair, bucking, but the strength of his grip on my hips keeps me close to him as he feasts like he's coming off a month-long fast.

"Kade..." My head jerks from side to side. "Taste... you." I want to taste him. Want to bring him at least a fraction of the pleasure he's bringing me, but all I manage to do is writhe and pull on his hair.

With a pop, I'm freed and drop my hands to his sturdy shoulders. Peppering my inner thigh with a flutter of soft kisses, he pulls the sensitive skin between his teeth. "Later."

Before I can protest, his hands and mouth are playing in concert with my tightly wound need, strumming my strings with the skill of a virtuoso. A guttural moan catapults from the deepest depths of my being, and a symphony of colors blasts forth, painting the black canvas behind my eyes in an intricate and vivid masterpiece.

"Kaaaade..." I roar over the explosion of sensations. There is no beginning, no ending. Time is a spiral of parallel universes and alternate dimensions. My body is not my own as I give way to the man cradling me in his arms.

"You're astounding." He places a gentle kiss on my temple.

And this time, when I shiver, it's not from the storm.

I groan at the blaring alarm and fumble for my phone, silencing it. My head aches from not enough sleep, but my body is satiated from last night's numerous orgasms. Turning my head, the euphoria flees at the sight of my empty bed.

"Shit." I punch the mattress then scrub my hands over my face. I shouldn't be upset or surprised, and yet... I'm both. The connection between Kade and me last night felt real and unbreakable, like we'd be waking up together this morning and every morning after. Throwing my arm over my eyes to shield the incoming sun that always manages to peek through my blinds, I lie in bed contemplating calling out sick because the queasy quake in my stomach is genuine. But then I bolt up. Nose twitching like a hound dog's, I sniff the air and jump out of bed.

Coffee. The scent of coffee filters into my room. I snatch a pair of shorts off the floor and hop into them while trying to walk and nearly face-plant into the wall in my excitement. If there's coffee, there's bound to be Kade. My chest swells as I make my way to the kitchen.

When I get there, I find... nothing. But for the gurgling coffee maker, it's empty. I glance back at the living room to make sure I didn't miss anything. It, too, is empty. The bathroom door is open, displaying it is unoccupied also. My chest deflates, and numbly, I pull a mug from the open shelf above the coffee pot. As I pour the coffee, I spy a two-by-two orange sticky note on the backsplash. My heart speeds up only to crash when I read the three words written in block letters, *See you Sat. - K.*

Well, shit...

Soggy tuna fish sandwich in hand, I peer at my computer screen. I've been looking at the same equation for the last twenty minutes, and still, all I can think about is how I'm more upset about waking up without Kade than I am about Storm. Don't get me wrong, I'm pissed Storm lied. And that bullshit about me mistaking *serious* for *exclusive*? Puh-lease... that's just semantics.

I'd be lying to myself if I didn't admit that there had been a niggle at the base of my skull every time Storm asked me to keep things quiet about the two of us. He said he wanted to keep his private life private. That he didn't want me to be hassled by fans and viewers. So, even though something about his rationale felt off—let's face it, he's a local meteorologist, not Beyoncé—I respected his wishes and endured the good-natured teasing from my rugby teammates about my imaginary boyfriend.

But the warm gushy sensation in my gut every time I recall Kade makes me think Plato was on to something with his musings that philia born out of eros is the best kind of friendship. Together, the two types of love are transformative.

Over the last year, Kade and I have developed a friendship, but after last night, I want more time with him. All morning I've wished for one more night, one more week, one more year...

"Hey, East. Have you seen Aileene around?" Cam's jovial voice takes me from my meanderings.

I drop the sandwich into the stainless-steel sandwich container and wipe my hands on my cloth napkin. "She said she'd be working in the small lab for most of the day. Something about an idea for the spray-on condom."

"Thanks, man." He pats my shoulder on his way to find his sister but stops, slowly turning and studying me. "Is everything okay?"

Cam is one of the most genuine people I've ever met. So, when he asks the question, his eyes searching, and everything in his demeanor saying he's ready to listen, I can't help but spill it all out.

"Last night, Kade and I found out we were dating the same guy. We went and confronted him, and he was with *another* guy. Then Kade came back to my place, and we..." I lift my shoulder. "He was gone when I woke this morning." Picking up my sandwich to have something to do with my hands, I bring it to my mouth but toss it back before taking a bite. "I'm sorry. None of that is appropriate work conversation."

Looking a little shell-shocked, Cam rolls a chair over and plops his big body down in front of me. "First, you seemed off, which is why I asked if you were okay. Second, I wouldn't have asked if I didn't want to know. Third, you've worked here long enough to know this company is about family." Elbows on knees, he leans forward. "You and Kade..." His dark blond brows wiggle up and down, his green eyes dancing with delight. "It's about time."

Straightening, I tilt my head. "What's that supposed to mean?"

"It means you two have been eying each other for a long time." Leaning back, he rests his right ankle on his left knee, his pink horse socks on display. "I get that the timing was off for a while with one of you dating someone when the other wasn't. But I never understood why you didn't go for it when the two of you were both single."

I wanted to, and the day I had worked up the courage to ask him out, Greer, one of the newer guys on our rugby team, had mentioned he was interested in Kade. "Greer expressed an interest." Not wanting to see the rebuke painting Cam's face, I rub at the line of blue ink on my thumb. "I didn't want to cause any friction on the team."

"So, even though you were into Kade and he was into you, you didn't ask him out because Greer, who has been hot for just about everyone on your team, my team, *and* anyone who stops by to watch, mentioned he was interested?" Letting the question hang in the air, his face placid, Cam waits with the patience only the father of a young child has, for me to conclude for myself how idiotic I sound.

Smoothing out the picture sitting on my desk that Olive drew for me yesterday, and I have yet to hang up, I suck my bottom lip between my teeth and try to avoid his gaze. "When you put it like that..."

Cam drops his foot to the floor and leans in with the same intensity I've witnessed on the pitch. "Easton, you are one of the kindest people I know, but you have got to stop acting like what you want doesn't matter. If you want the thing with Kade to be more than one night, tell him."

"But if he doesn't want the same thing, it could make things on the team awkward, and I don't want that." Not to mention, I'm not sure I could handle rejection from him. The way he held me and distracted me from the storm... It felt like he was invested, not a feeling one gets from a one-night stand.

"Fuck the team."

My eyes bulge because we all know Cam's devotion to everyone who plays in the league is unwavering.

He holds up his hand before I can argue. "What I mean is, don't use the team as an excuse. So what if things get weird for a little bit? It will work itself out. Neither you nor Kade does drama. Heck, Aspen can barely stand me, but we don't let it interfere with practices or league events."

I don't say anything about how we all have bets on when Aspen and Cam will get together. The sexual tension between them is palpable. When they argue, there's more heat and steam than a shower scene in any porno I've seen. Instead, I voice my real concern. "But what if last night was just a rebound thing? What if it meant more to me than it did to him?"

"And what if he's asking himself the same thing?" Cam rises from the chair and straightens his pale pink tie with hot pink polka dots. "Haven't you ever noticed how Kade lingers around practice until you leave? Or how he saves a seat for you when we go out for drinks after a game? Or how he seems to always partner with you during practices?"

"Yeah, but we're friends." Feeling fidgety, I tug on the cuff of my sleeve as I struggle with what can only be a rugby ball lodged in my throat.

Cam's expression is one of indulgent annoyance. "And maybe he'd like something more. Talk to him, East. Do something for yourself for once."

Dumping the rest of my uneaten sandwich in the trash bin, I consider Cam and what he said as he makes his way in search of his sister. For a year, I've gotten to know Kade, and the more I know, the more I like him. And yes, the first time those green eyes took me in, I was hooked. But he's so much more than his good looks. He's carefree without being careless. He's spontaneous but unhurried. He's intelligent and perceptive and insightful.

Perhaps Cam's right. Maybe I need to tell Kade how I feel, and what I want.

Right, that's what I'll do. But first I need a plan.

Bolstered by my new resolve, I move my finger across the mouse pad and bring my monitor to life. I have two days until our game to figure out how to broach the topic, and the best way to present the information. I just hope I don't walk away dejected because if Kade rejects me, I may crumble.

Chapter Four

♥

Kade

My stomach tightens with every step I take toward the sun-drenched field. Clutching the strap of my gear bag and my travel mug, I force my feet to keep moving, focusing on the blades of grass, trying to ignore the way my heart is pounding.

Scanning my teammates congregating by the bleachers, I spy Easton on the sidelines, crouched beside Cam's daughter, Olive. He tucks the yellow dandelion she hands him behind his ear. The gesture is so sweet, such an *Easton* thing to do, my heart aches even while my nerves swell.

I press the coffee mug against my sternum. It's been two days—both the longest and shortest two days of my life—since I've seen him, and I'm not prepared for the one-two punch of need and desire, or for what to say to him. Or, for what he might say to me...

Leaving his bed so early Thursday morning hadn't been easy, but I had a full day's worth of repairs waiting for me at the shop and couldn't linger. Waking him after he had such trouble sleeping due to the storm seemed cruel and incredibly selfish, so I didn't.

Telling myself he needed adequate rest was a convenient excuse, a cover for my fear that he'd wake up, see me, and have regrets. Fear rushes through me now, twisting like thousands of tiny knives with each step that brings me closer to the pitch and my teammates.

We're playing against the over-thirty team today. I wave to Mateo and Cam as I keep to the sidelines and make my way to the bleachers. Both teams are taking the field now for warmups. I need to hustle. My coffee sloshes out of the mug's opening, sending tan rivulets over the back of my hand. Several of my teammates wave as I drop my bag and mug and sit to exchange my sneakers for cleats. Meeting Easton's gaze, I fumble my sneaker lace, knotting it. Heat blooms into my cheeks. He doesn't smile, just holds me captive with his study.

"Kade, let's go," Aspen calls from where he's leading our guys in the warmups.

Damn it.

I concentrate on switching to the proper footwear, then scramble to join the team. As I drop into the exercises, Easton's presence pulls me like a magnet, keeping me aware of him no matter where I move my body. So much so that

I lose my balance during the walking lunges and end up swaying like I've lost my equilibrium. Without Easton, I feel like I have. I'm a mess.

In the small space of time between warmups and the game's start, Greer is beside me, chatting about the new guy he's dating. I'm trying to be a supportive friend, but my focus is fractured by Easton. His attention is dominated by Olive and her two sidekicks, Mateo's niece and nephew. The kids are adorable, and Easton is so sweet with them. He glances at me twice, and I can't tell if he wants to talk. His expression gives nothing away. In the two days since we were together, while I agonized over every possibility, he hasn't called or texted me, hasn't acknowledged the note I left or our time together. I'm certain he regrets what we did. I don't want to lose him as a friend and also don't know how to navigate being with him on this team in the aftermath.

On the field, I get into position. All around me, my teammates and opponents are lining up. Playful trash talk flies. The whistle blows. The ball is drop-kicked and arcs into the field. I spring into action, pumping my legs as fast as I can. Easton sprints past me, dark hair flopping onto his forehead, jersey molded to his skin. Watching him, I continue forward... and miss my chance to take down Mateo. He blows by me. I pivot, but not fast enough. In a series of coordinated movements, the over-thirty team gets the ball to Cam and he crosses our try zone and touches the ball to the ground for a try.

We've been playing for less than a minute, and they're already five points ahead. Sucking in air, I watch the conversion kick sail through the posts and above the bar. The kick is good, giving them an extra two points.

Disgusted with myself for being too distracted to do anything defensively to prevent that try, I line up again. Play resumes. Easton's presence continues to tug at me, splintering my focus as I race across the field.

Fifteen minutes in, and I'm getting looks of concern from my teammates and opponents. I haven't played so poorly since the first weeks of my first season, when I was still learning the rules and basics. Rubbing my hands over my face, overheated from running and from embarrassment, I take a breath. The scent of the coffee clinging to my hand mocks me with memories of Thursday and how I started the caffeinated brew for Easton and spent way too much time in his perfectly styled kitchen agonizing over what to say in the note I was leaving. So much time that the blaring of his alarm clock jolted my heart into my throat and nearly knocked me on my ass as I bolted to his front door, pockets filled with crumpled up, discarded scribblings that revealed too much.

"Kade!" Aspen yells from behind me.

Jerking my head and twisting my torso in his direction, I miss the ball flying toward me. Cam barrels in and swipes it to his chest. Pivoting, I lunge, throwing myself at his legs, but he eludes my grasp. I slam into the grass, empty-handed.

Things don't improve. I'm consistently a step off. No matter how hard I try to block out everything but the game, I can't.

At halftime, I follow my teammates off the field. Hesitating by the bleachers, watching Easton in the corner of my vision, I don't know which way to go. Toward him? Away?

"Kade." Wiping a towel over his face, Aspen catches hold of my shoulder and steers me past the far end of the bleachers. We come to a stop beyond the listening range of my teammates. Blue eyes lined with slashes of sparkling copper search my face. The warm color is echoed in his ombre-dyed red to orange to blond hair, but every shade is overshadowed by the concern clouding his gaze. "Are you not feeling well?"

Guilt triples the size of the pit in my stomach. "I'm sorry I missed the ball and those tackles."

"That doesn't answer my question. Are you ill? It's hot today, is the heat getting to you? Do you need to sit out the second half? We can have Wyatt or Greer sub for you for the rest of the game."

I can't deny I've played like shit. That's not helping my teammates. They deserve my best. The laughter and teasing trash-talk between them and the over-thirties fills the air. "I'll be better. I'm sorry."

He lays his hand on my forehead. "You don't feel like you have a fever."

"I'm not sick. I was just... distracted." Sighing, I shove my hands into the pockets of my shorts as he lowers his hand. "I want to play."

Blue eyes spear into mine, assessing my screw-up self for a long moment. Aspen is so perceptive, so aware of what's going on with the members of our team, I doubt he's missed Easton's and my vibe today. The temptation to turn and look for Easton is almost overwhelming. "You know you can talk to me about anything."

"I know. And thanks." Hoping to relieve my friend's worries, I force a smile. East and I aren't the first team-mates who have been involved. Some of the other pairings have worked out, but others have caused chaos and drama within the team. I don't want that to happen.

Mateo, one of the players on the over-thirty team, jogs toward us, brow crinkled as he zeroes in on me. At thirty-seven, he is eleven years older than me and is like the older brother I never had. "Everything all right?"

My nod is as false as my smile. "Sure. Why?"

His frown deepens as he hands me my water bottle. "Because you were uncharacteristically distracted the entire first half."

"Since you're my opposition, shouldn't you be happy about that?"

Mateo shares a look with Aspen that rides the thin line between concern and worry and then they stand shoulder to shoulder, pinning me in place. I don't think anything, including the whistle to start the match's second half, could pull them away. "I want to win, but you're obviously not okay. Talk to us."

They're more than friends to me. They're family. Not for the first time, I'm grateful our two teams get along so well and that through our shared practices, I've gained a solid support system and damn good friends. Maybe I do need to get this out, to give voice to the fears, and then maybe I'll be able to concentrate and won't continue to wreck my team's chances at a comeback. "After practice on Wednesday, Easton and I found out the same guy was seeing us behind our backs. We dumped him then ended up back at East's place, and we, well... got together."

Mateo and Aspen share another look, but I can't decipher this one. They both take a step closer to me and Mateo lays a gentle hand on my shoulder. "While my first inclination is to say that I'm happy for you two, and we all expected it to happen at some point, you don't seem happy. Why not?"

"I'm afraid he thinks it's a mistake."

Aspen whips his head, peering over his shoulder to where Easton has to be standing. "Why? What did he say?"

The uncertainty and discomfort that has lain over me the past few days increases. I desperately want it gone. "I kind of left before he woke up. We haven't spoken yet."

That laser-focus is back on me, as unyielding as high beams on a one lane road, and I don't have any options to steer out of the path of Aspen's scrutiny. "You've got to be kidding me. Why haven't you talked to him?"

I drag the toe of my cleat through the grass. Concentrating on the way the blades part is easier than looking at my friends. "I didn't want to hear him say that he regretted it."

"*Kade*." Aspen's voice is all exasperation.

"I know. I'm a coward."

Mateo nudges my arm until I look up again. He's serious and intense and one of the toughest, strongest people I know. Whenever he speaks, I've learned to listen. His words carry the weight of wisdom and experience. "You're definitely not a coward. You've never held back from going after what you want before, so why start now?"

I give the water bottle my full attention, turning it over and over. The sloshing of the water matches the churning in my stomach. "What if he thinks I don't measure up?"

Mateo takes the bottle from my grasp. "In what way?"

Gaze pinging from Aspen to him, I lower my voice in case the wind could carry it to Easton. "From what I've seen and heard, he dates professionals. Guys who are established, who have their lives together. Not someone who jumps from job to job and place to place and spent his first year in Philly couch-surfing. He's a freaking scientist. He wears suits to work. And have you *seen* his apartment? It's like something in a magazine ad or decorator's portfolio."

"You don't give yourself enough credit." Mateo's voice is gentle, the same tone he uses when he's talking to his niece or nephew. "Having a perfectly decorated home or staying in the same job for several years doesn't determine someone's worth."

"I know that."

"Do you?" Aspen challenges me with a raised brow and an edge to his voice that only creeps in when he's about to get riled up. "Then why are you selling yourself short?"

"It's different."

"How?"

My hands clutch fistfuls of air. Restlessness flares, but I can't run away from my worries. I shove my hands into my pockets again. "Because this is *me*. I like him so much and want there to be an *us*, so much."

Mateo moves in a step closer. He presses the water bottle into my chest, right over my aching heart. "What if he feels the same way?"

My fingers feel clumsy on the bottle, but I grasp hold and clutch it like an anchor. "What if he doesn't? Leaping into things hasn't always worked out well for me. I don't want to hurt Easton or be hurt by him."

"Kade..." Mateo exchanges another look with Aspen before they both focus on me, arms crossed over their chests, wearing identical, no-nonsense, zero-bullshit expressions. "Aspen and I have known Easton for four years longer than you. We've seen how you've helped draw him out of his shell. You. No one else. He seems more relaxed, happier, when you're there."

"Exactly," Aspen adds. "His gaze always seeks you out first. If you're not here, he asks where you are. He opens up, lights up, around you. When he's with you, he shines. And you do too, with him."

Digesting their words, I step back until I can see Easton on the sidelines. He always seems to shine to me, brighter than anyone else. Do I really have that much of an effect on him? Do I really make him light up? When I'm with him, I always feel lighter inside.

Mateo lays his hand on my shoulder, the touch warm, and solid, and comforting. "Courage is feeling the fear about something and doing it anyway. If you want him, tell him. Show him. With great risk comes great reward, right?"

"Right... Well, sometimes. Other times, great risk leaves you with nothing to show for it or with an incredible loss." So many of my life experiences, ideas, whims, and efforts have resulted in dreams turning to dust. But I work up a smile for my friend. "Don't worry, I know where you're going with that."

"Good. Now, I need to get back to my team, and so do you two. Halftime is almost over."

I nod. The fear and nerves trilling through my body have been tempered by the warmth of gratitude and friendship. "Thanks, Teo."

His smile is full of support as he squeezes my shoulder. "Anytime."

After Mateo jogs away, Aspen drapes his arm over my shoulder. "We have about thirty seconds before the second half begins. If you want to play, you can. If you want to sit out, that's fine."

"I want to play. If I screw up again, I won't force you to make the call. I'll take myself out of the game. Okay?"

"Whatever you need to do so that you're prepared to talk to East." He leads me toward the bleachers. At the other end, surrounded by the kids, Easton is talking to Cam. My heart begins racing.

"I can't talk to him now. There isn't time."

As if Aspen can feel my spiraling, he pulls me into a half-hug. "After the game. You can hold on until then. You've got this, Kade."

I hug him back, clinging tight for a moment, feeling so lucky that after years of wandering, I finally ended up finding my place, and the solid relationships I've come to depend on. "Thanks."

"As Teo said, anytime." His hug turns full and fierce and he thumps my back twice before pulling away. I can't shift my gaze from Easton. The tap of Aspen's pink sports drink against my water bottle startles me. His smile is encouraging and understanding, but a hint of concern remains. "Ready? Let's play."

Cam and Easton make their way onto the pitch. Other players follow. I drop my water beside Aspen's drink and then walk with him to our spots. My insides feel like jelly. I don't know how I'll get through the next forty minutes intact.

The game resumes, and I'm still distracted. So much so that after a dropped ball, missed tackle, and incurring a penalty, I pull myself and let Greer sub for me for the rest of the game.

The minutes tick by. From my place on the bench, I feel the weight of Easton's stare. He glances at me every chance he gets and my heart tugs each time. I need to talk to him, to tell him how I feel, to be brave.

When the game ends, I gather my stuff and move to wait by Easton's bag at the far end of the bench. Waving goodbye to Olive, who is headed off for a playdate with Mateo's sister's kids, I force a smile and try to pretend that things are normal, and I'm not about to risk a broken heart.

He approaches me slowly, warily, brows raised. "Hey."

My ears grow hot and my stomach churns. Rubbing my hand over the back of my neck, I blurt out, "I owe you a pad of sticky notes."

"What?" Brows scrunching together, Easton tilts his head, peering at me like I'm spouting nonsense. Hair mussed, skin gleaming with sweat, he looks amazing.

"I used so many—" I shake my head and wave away the nerves-sparked statement. "That's not important. I need to talk to you. About what happened on Wednesday."

Easton squares his shoulders and splays his legs wider like he's bracing himself. "All right."

Movement beyond his shoulder catches my attention. Mateo, Cam, and Aspen are watching us from the sidelines. The rest of our teammates are milling around near them. I don't love having an audience, but I can't put off this conversation any longer. Focusing on Easton once more, on those brown eyes watching me so carefully, I wonder if he can hear my heart pounding. "It meant something to me. Being with you."

The lines in his face ease, but don't disappear. "For me too."

Relief rushes in, crashing over the nervous swells, leaving me unsteady. "Yeah?"

He nods, biting his lip. Too much of his wariness remains. "Yeah. I thought maybe we were starting something, but then you were gone."

"I left a note." I take a step closer, but feel like a coward again.

"*See you Saturday* was pretty vague regarding your feelings."

Frustrated with myself, past and current, I drag my hands through my hair. "I know. I tried writing that note so many times. I didn't know what to say. How to tell you that I wanted more. There are over a dozen discarded versions in my recycling bin at home."

Easton shifts closer to me, almost near enough for me to touch him. "So why don't you tell me what one of those versions said?"

The halting words I'd written swim through my mind, but what surfaces is the memory of Thursday's early morning hours. "When I was holding you that night, while the thunder and lightning raged, I didn't want to let go. I barely slept, wanting to make sure you were okay, but as I laid there, I kept thinking about how we're different. And how big those differences are. You're so together. Your home, your job... The guys you typically date are like that too. I was sure that, in the light of day, you'd tell me that I'm a drifter who hasn't found his purpose yet, and that we'd made a mistake."

Shaking his head, Easton takes my hand, surrounding it with warmth. Being touched by him again is overwhelming. "Kade, you're one of the smartest, bravest people I know. You can read or see something once and commit it to memory. One of the things that first drew me to you was your background, all of the places you've been, all of the things you've seen and done. You have the courage to try new things and the guts to walk away when something isn't making you happy. When I look at you, those qualities are what I think about. I've worried that I'm too boring for you."

"Never." I link our fingers together, loving the way they fit. That magnetic pull I've felt all afternoon is stronger now. Irresistible. Only one fear remains. "I want *us* so much. I don't want to be a rebound, to lose you if you're not ready for a relationship right now, after what happened with Storm. So, I can wait for you, East. For as long as you need."

"Three months with Storm wasn't a long amount of time. And to be completely honest with you," gaze searching mine, Easton closes the distance between us. "I've been falling for you since we met. Have wanted to be with you for nearly that long too. I want you, Kade. Not for a night, or a weekend, not something casual, and not a fling. For the long term."

The words thaw something inside me that's been frozen since Wednesday night. Holding tight to Easton's hand, I slide my other arm around him. The fingers of his free hand trace along my cheek. We stare at each other, smiling, basking, and then we're moving as one, coming together.

The feel of his lips against my mouth weakens me in the best way. I soak up every sensation. His scent: sunscreen, laundry detergent, and sweat. His body: the warmth of his length against me, the way his arms are banding like he can't hold me close enough, and the press of his lips, soft yet firm. His taste: the lemon sports drink he favors along with his unique flavor.

I could go on kissing him forever, but fresh voices are gathering by the bleachers. There's another match starting soon and the teams are arriving.

Easton gentles the kiss. "We need to go."

"I know." I tease the words over his lips. Drawing back, I can't stop myself from threading my fingers through his hair. A glance at the sidelines confirms the rest of our teammates are gone. "Do you want to go to the pub with the rest of the guys?"

"I think we should, for a little while, so they don't worry about us. I got *a lot* of questions from them today... Then we can go back to your place. Or my place. Wherever you'll be the most comfortable." Easton tugs me to sit on the lowest bleacher row. I realize we're still wearing our cleats. He switches his cleats for sneakers, and I do the same.

"Honestly, being with you is where I'm most comfortable." Shouldering both of our gear bags, I take his hand and pull him to standing.

His smile is beautiful. "I feel the same way."

Hand in hand, we stroll along the sidelines, heading toward the sidewalk. I spare one glance at the field's parking lot to check on my bike. I always leave it there when grabbing beers post-game because the pub is only a short walk away.

Short enough that our teammates should be *there*, and not *here*, at the field's edge, crowding the sidewalk, waiting for us. But here they are.

They erupt into cheers, applauding and whistling, and a few call out, "About time!"

Confused, I look at Aspen, who is cheering as loud as all the rest. "What's going on?"

Before he can answer, Cam, grinning, strides toward him, palm held out. "I win. Time to pay up."

"What's going on?" I ask again. Easton shrugs, while Aspen takes out his phone and types into it.

Beside us, Mateo finally puts an end to my curiosity. "There's been a pool going since last season for the two of you, bets on when you'd finally get together. Cam picked today."

Easton and I stare at each other in shock. Then his brows narrow as he focuses on Cam. "Really? How convenient."

Cam's phone chimes. I catch a glimpse of the screen, open to the digital wallet app we use to send in our dues, but not the amount of money Aspen sent him. He pockets the phone, not the least bit repentant. "Hey, East, I didn't tell you to specifically wait until today to talk it out with Kade. But I'm happy you did."

Still not quite believing this is happening, I glance at Mateo. "You were in on the pool too?"

"Yeah, but my day came and went last season."

Trying to reconcile that nugget with his and Aspen's advice during halftime, I look at my team captain. "And you?"

Aspen grins. "Someone had to organize it."

"Hey, I helped with organizing." Cam's words and attention are solely on Aspen.

"I can't believe this," I say to Easton and he nods. Actually, I *can* believe it, considering the pool the rest of us have going for Aspen and Cam, who are now bickering about which of them actually organized the pool for Easton and me.

"You're impossible." Shaking his head, Aspen levels a stare at Cam that would shrivel a lesser man.

Cam merely grins then blows him a kiss. "Relax. I'll use my winnings to buy everyone drinks at the pub."

Mateo steps between them like a referee. "Great idea. Let's go. We need to celebrate Easton and Kade, and we're taking up too much of the sidewalk."

His words get the rest of the guys moving and his arms around Aspen and Cam's shoulders force them to fall in step with him. Easton pulls me forward and one block later, we're in the pub, and Cam has bought pitchers of beer, food, and special drinks for everyone.

Surrounded by our friends, sitting beside Easton with my arm around his shoulder the way I always longed to do during our outings with the team, I'm filled with so many good feelings.

Easton lays his head on my shoulder. "I can't believe we're here, like this. You and me."

"You and me," I repeat, thrilled by the thought. The three words, when linked together, mean everything to me. They tie Easton and me together, signifying that we're committed to each other, that we're giving into the bond that our hearts realized early on.

He raises his head and smiles at me with lips shiny from his drink. "When I arrived at practice on Wednesday, I had no idea the way things would spiral. It's been a wild ride, but I wouldn't change any part because it ended with you and me together."

"If I *could* change any part, I would've stayed on Thursday morning. Hashed things out then." My fingers tighten on his shoulder. I draw him closer to my side and press a kiss to his temple. "But since I can't go back and change things, I'll make it up to you. Starting tomorrow morning."

Smiling, Easton traces his fingertip along my cheek. "I like that plan. Waking up together. Starting this relationship the way it should be, with coffee in bed."

"I'll bring you as many cups as you can handle," I promise as I lean in, desperate to taste his lips.

He feathers his lips over mine, teasing me with the softest and lightest of touches before angling his head and kissing me deeper. His other hand is laying over my heart and I capture it there. After all, it belongs to him. I know he'll guard it and keep it safe, just as I'll do with his.

When breathing becomes necessary, we raise our heads, but I keep hold of our hands. The shimmering bliss in his gaze echoes in me, spanning out until I'm sure everyone in the pub can feel our happiness.

I can't wait to see where things with us will lead, and I know that we'll give each other everything as we embrace our future together.

Epilogue

♥

Easton

I GROAN AT THE blaring *beep beep beep* of a truck backing up on the streets below my bedroom window. Slitting an eye open, I peek at the clock and groan again. Seven AM on a *Sunday*. Why must they be so loud this early on the weekend?

My head aches from not enough sleep, but my body is satiated from last night's numerous orgasms. Grinning at the memory of Kade's mouth exploring every inch of my skin, the stroke of his fingers along my stiff shaft and down the crease of my ass, the exhilaration of coming together and knowing he'll be here in the morning, I stretch and reach for him.

Only to be greeted with the cool creases of empty sheets. Turning my head, euphoria flees at the sight of my empty bed.

"Shit." I punch the mattress then scrub my hands over my face. A cloud of dismay smothers the bliss of seconds ago as my ribs constrict, making every breath burn. After all the reassurances we whispered to each other, the confessions of attraction and connection, the promises of this being something long and lasting, our bond seemed established, secure, unbreakable. I thought we'd be waking up together this morning and every morning after.

Throwing my arm over my eyes to shield the sting of tears pricking them, I fend off the cloud of disappointment threatening to shatter the belief that I could rely on Kade. His words, his touch, they bolstered the hope that *my* person was out there, and that person was Kade.

But in a reckless about-face, my disillusion transforms into anger, massacring all rational thoughts of examining the situation thoroughly. The only question I can form is, how best to maim Kade.

Okay, *maim* may be too strong a word, I don't *really* want to physically injure him. But right now, I want him to feel at least a fraction of the devastation bludgeoning my core because with Kade, I believed what he said, believed he was different.

"That's it." I punch the mattress again. I'm done with men promising one thing, like serving you coffee in bed, and not following through. Done with trusting.

I am done.

Period.

But then I bolt up, my nose twitching. Coffee. He said he'd make coffee and would bring it to me in bed. I don't smell it, but I was too distracted last night to prepare the coffee pot for this morning. And Kade won't know where the coffee grinder is or where I store the beans. He's probably in the kitchen trying to find them.

My belly flutters with hope, driving away doubt and the queasy quake that have been churning in it. Jumping out of bed, I snatch a pair of shorts from the floor and hop into them, nearly face-planting into the wall in my rush to the kitchen.

When I get there, I find... nothing. The coffee maker stands silent. The mug I used yesterday morning is still in its place on the drying rack. Everything is exactly as I left it. I glance back at the living room and bathroom to find they are both vacant. Scanning the backsplash for a note, my chest deflates.

Nothing.

Numbly, I locate the coffee grinder and, with shaking hands, scoop beans into it. Disbelief stabs me with the savagery of a murderous thief.

He left.

Kade left.

And this time, he didn't even bother to leave a note.

I push the button to the grinder and watch as the blades pulverize the beans until they are nothing more than fine bits of umber dust. My thoughts swirl, cacophonous and grating. Even the pulsating sound of coffee beans being mashed and pounded is unable to deafen them.

Today, I will brood, and maybe even sulk, but tomorrow I will—

A hand comes down on my left shoulder, and I jolt. Without thinking, I grab the perpetrator's wrist with my right hand. Being too close to the countertop to toss him forward, I seize a finger, yanking it as far back as I can while using my body to push him backward and free myself.

The intruder grunts and falls away with a thud. "Fuck, East."

Blood racing, head thumping, I spin on my heel.

Eyes wide with disbelief and lying sprawled out on his back, holding his finger, is Kade. Beautiful, gorgeous Kade.

"Shit. Sorry." I drop to my knees, touching his face, his chest, his legs. Everything appears to be in place. "Are you okay?"

His mouth lops to one side. "I think you broke my finger."

"Oh my god." The jumble of emotions that have been competing for control since I woke to an empty bed churn into a ball of guilt, gashing my chest with every bounce. I cup his hand in both of mine, squeezing his pointer. "I'm so sorry. Does this hurt? Let me get you ice." I release his hand, but before I can pop to my feet, Kade tugs me to him and kisses me.

His lips are warm and tender, and he tastes of mint and a hint of bitter caramel. I sigh, molding my body to the hard planes of his. The prick from the hair on his legs as they pin mine between them and the scrape of his beard against my cheek as he swirls his tongue along the rim of my ear excites and entices. As is evident by the awakening of my hungry cock.

Framing my face with his hands, his bright eyes dart between mine. "What was the take-down about?"

The burn of embarrassment rushes from the tips of my toes to the top of my ears. My head falls forward to Kade's shoulder, and when I attempt to move, his legs tighten, keeping me in place. The slow, steady movement of his hand rubbing figure-eights on my back quiets the urge to change my name and move to a new country rather than admit what an overacting, untrusting idiot I am.

Opening my eyes, I spot the grape I dropped yesterday but couldn't find under the refrigerator. "I thought you'd left."

"I did. To get coffee." The huskiness of his words vibrates through my chest, taunting me for being so stupid.

"For good. I thought you left for good, so I wasn't prepared for anyone else to be here." I rub my itchy nose. My admission is a jab to everything we assured each other of last night.

The figure-eights cease. Shifting to his elbows, his brows rise, then drop and squish together, bewildered by my confession.

I roll off him and onto my back, keeping my eyes trained on the ceiling. I can't look at him. Don't want to witness the moment his confusion morphs into disappointment.

"East..." My name is spoken with such tenderness I can't help but turn my head in his direction. "Baby..."

His term of endearment blasts a surge of euphoria through me, and I bite down on my bottom lip to keep from asking him to say it again.

Baby is familiar.

Baby is personal.

Baby is... intimate.

Pulling me to sit, he skims his fingers through my hair and pushes it off my forehead. "Didn't you see the note I left?"

"No."

Rising to his knees, he surveys the countertop. "Huh." He stands and looks in the sink. "I left it here." He points to the backsplash. "I was hoping to be back before you woke up." He bends down searching for the elusive note, then stands, hands on his hips. "It's not here."

"But you are." I get up and thread my arms around his waist. "You're here."

He tugs me closer, dropping his hands to my ass. "I am. Just like I told you I would be. Just like we agreed." He squeezes my cheeks with enough force to send a perfect prick of pain hurling up my spine. "Are we going to have to review what we discussed last night?"

"It was a good discussion." I wiggle my brows and grind my pelvis into him, revived by the relief that he's not pissed at the conclusion I jumped to with only flimsy, circumstantial evidence.

Much to the disappointment of my cock, he releases me with a quick peck on the lips. "Before we *discuss* anything, you're going back to bed."

"But I'm awake, and I need coffee."

"And I'm going to bring you coffee. *In bed*." He points toward the bedroom. "Get your sexy ass in there so I can do what I promised."

For the first time in forever, I'm unfettered. Liberated by Kade. Able to breathe fully, I relish the loosening of my muscles and realize I've always carried a level of tension in them, but with Kade, it evaporates.

"Hurry up. I stopped at the bakery and picked up pastries too." He snaps the waistband of my shorts, his green eyes playful and eager. "And lose the shorts. I want you like you were before I left this morning."

Head as light as my weightless body, I bask in the knowledge that we're okay, and I chuckle. "You're ridiculous."

"And you love it." He flashes me one of his irresistible smiles, and I dissolve faster than sugar in warm water.

"I do." His rich laughter chases me as I rush down the hallway, yanking my shorts off in a hurry to my bedroom. Tossing my shorts to the corner, I dive into bed and pull the sheets over my naked body.

My chest leaps and plummets with every breath as I peer at the doorway, awaiting the arrival of the man who has been my joy since I met him. And now he's really mine.

Kade

Searching the freezer for an ice pack for my throbbing hand, I listen to Easton's footsteps as he hurries to the bedroom.

I will never forget the mixture of embarrassment and hesitation that clouded his features when he admitted that he'd thought I'd skipped out on him. I hate that anything at all ruined the sweet and sexy morning I'd envisioned for us, but especially for it to have been his erroneous thought that I'd ever want to willingly walk away from him.

The small circular ice pack in the freezer door should work for what I need. Spying a pair of heat resistant oven gloves atop the counter, I slide one over my hand to keep the pack in place at the joint where my finger meets my palm so I can get breakfast ready unencumbered. I don't think my finger is broken after all, but something—whether a muscle, tendon, or ligament, I don't yet know—feels strained. Still, I'm happy to know that East can easily take care of himself, not that I doubted it before this morning.

A glance at the spot where I laid on the floor, and another to the hall leading to his bedroom, and I'm determined to find that sticky note. Paper does not simply disappear into thin air. It's not on the floor, not on the backsplash. Perhaps it somehow fluttered under the fridge or behind the oven?

I reach over the coffeemaker to unplug the coffee grinder. The plug falls behind the machine and the rustling crinkle that follows is not the sound of rubber or plastic hitting the stone counter.

Shoving the coffeemaker to the side reveals the bright orange note had fallen behind it.

Shaking my head, I huff a laugh and apply the note to the top of the to-go cup that has Easton's coffee.

The need to get into the bedroom so I can finally be with him quickens my movements. I find a breadboard that can double as a tray, and take a white stoneware dinner plate from the cabinet. The sugary and buttery scents of the custard-filled cornetto, chocolate croissant, apple turnover, blueberry crumble bar, cinnamon donut, and lemon blackberry scone I bought fill the air as I remove them from the bakery bag, plate them in a circle, and slice them in half for easy sharing. Adding napkins and our coffees completes the tray.

Carrying the meal, I tread a quiet path to the bedroom, as I would have if I'd arrived back here before Easton had woken up.

Sunlight spills through the sides of the blinds, casting patterns on the floor. I can't help smiling at him lying there. His back is to me, the lines of muscle are gorgeous, and with the light hitting them, he's posed in an intimate portrait for me alone.

"Time to wake up, Easton." My voice is soft as I pad farther into the room.

Rolling over, he grins at me. "Are we really doing this?"

"Yes. I want everything to be as perfect as possible. You deserve that. And zero doubts."

His grin shifts to a soft, shy smile. "All right then. And thank you."

"So, you'll play along?" I set the tray on the spot I vacated less than half an hour ago and begin stripping off my clothes.

Easton gives me an exaggerated stretch and feigns a yawn before gaping at me and doing a double take at the tray. "Morning. Oh, wow, what's all this?"

My lips twitching at his faux surprise, I slip onto the mattress and hand him the to-go cup. "I found the note behind the coffeemaker. It must have fallen off the back-splash."

He plucks the brilliant orange square from the lid and reads what I'd written out loud. "E, I'll be back in a few minutes with a surprise. xo, K."

My cheeks heat at the XO. It flowed from the pen as naturally as my initial. "I really wouldn't just leave, East. Not after all we talked about yesterday. I'm in this with you. One hundred percent. No place else I'd rather be."

Nodding, he presses the note to the tray, smoothing the paper flat against the wood. The embarrassed ducking of his head is back, and I can't have that. I gently stroke my fingers along his temple and into his hair. When he lifts his gaze to meet mine, I smile. I understand how things could have looked to him today, and I know he's been burned a few times, so I'll happily remind him of my commitment to him, to us, as often as he needs.

He sips the coffee and his eyes widen in honest surprise. "You know how I take my coffee?"

"Of course. Coconut creamer and a teaspoon of raw sugar." I lean in and tease my lips over his, tasting the coconut and coffee. "I pay attention to you."

"I know you do." Smile deepening, he lifts his hand to my cheek. The stroke of his thumb along my jaw is a slow, deliberate drag that scatters my pulse. "I'm happy you're here. That you stayed."

"I'd wake up beside you every morning if I could." Maybe I'm being too honest, revealing too much, too soon, but I can't help it. Easton deserves total honesty.

His thumb falters before continuing with the strokes. The openness of his gaze, the hope I see there, echoes with the wanting I feel deep in my soul. "Who says you can't?"

My breath catches and my heart beat grows wild. What I want is being dangled before me like a delicious, craved, rare treat. The room shrinks down to Easton. Only Easton. "Are you being serious?"

"Yes. I woke up thinking about that today. How right everything feels with you here." The hand cupping my face slides into my hair and gentle pressure guides me forward. Easton settles his mouth over mine.

The gesture and the words weaken me. I'd do anything for this man.

Anything.

Angling my head, I take the kiss deeper. Easton is warm and welcoming, and I want every morning to begin like this. Kissing each other, holding each other, being each other's steady support and soft place to land.

Drawing in a breath, I raise my head and brush his hair out of his beautiful face. "If we're going to be waking up together, we'll need to find sticky notes with stronger adhesive or get a bulletin board for notes so there's no further miscommunication."

With a rueful smile, he glances at my gloved hand. "I'm sorry about that. Can I kiss it better?"

I slip my hand free of the material, leaving the ice pack to rest inside. The area on my upper palm and lower half of my index finger is red from the cold, but the pain is almost gone. Easton captures my hand and raises it to his lips. He presses a kiss to my fingertip, then each knuckle along that digit, and finally my palm.

Closing my eyes at the sweetness he's offering, I bask in his attention. Every touch is healing on multiple levels. "Thank you."

"For what?" His voice is a whisper, teasing breath over my skin.

"The kiss. Caring. Wanting me here. Wanting me in general." Opening my eyes, I drink in the sight of Easton, holding my hand, gazing at me like I'm something special. My heart fills to overflowing. "I think you're amazing, East."

"I think you are too." Eyes shimmering, he presses my hand over his heart. The gesture reminds me of when he laid his hand over my heart yesterday at the pub, and I captured it there. I wonder if he's thinking about that too.

I slide my other arm around his shoulders, nestling him against me in the cool room. He may be able to protect himself from chance encounters with attackers, and hold his own on and off the rugby field, but he's still mine to protect. "I'll guard your heart. Keep it safe."

The hand holding mine tightens and Easton's heartbeat quickens under my palm. The shades of vulnerability shifting across his features give way to a look that is pure sunshine. "I know you will. And I'll do the same for you."

I think about all the trials and errors that eventually led me to Philly and to Easton. "I'm lucky I found you."

"I'm the lucky one." He nudges his shoulder into my torso. The playful curve of his cheeks and twinkle in his eyes suggests the time for serious talk is over. He's good and so am I, and we can go back to how the morning would have been if I'd arrived back here before he'd even realized that I'd gone. "Are all those treats for you, or can I persuade you to share?"

I shift the tray to rest halfway over both of our laps, then pick up my coffee. "I wasn't sure what you would be in the mood for, so I got a variety. I figured we could split each one."

He glances at each baked good and then raises a brow. "There's enough here that we might have enough fortification to stay in until dinner."

"A day in bed with you? Yes, please." I swipe my finger along the custard poking out of the center of the cornetto and dot it on the center of Easton's lower lip. Then lean in and take my time licking it off.

His hungry groan feeds me and the urgency of his answering kiss, the tease of tongue, the firm, coaxing lips, spikes my blood with a need, voracious and potent, that only Easton can quench.

He pulls back, breathless, and grins. "Ready to eat?"

I'm ready for so many things. More kissing. More sex. Talking. Laughing. Holding him. Weaving our lives together. But breakfast is a good start. "What do you want to try first?"

Coffee in one hand, he sips it as he breaks off a piece of the cinnamon donut and raises it to my lips. The dough is soft and the spice dances on my tastebuds.

I lift one half of the apple turnover and hold it up for Easton to taste. With a moan and a nod of approval, he chews the bite.

Relaxing against soft pillows, wrapped in soft sheets, I lean against Easton. In between sips of coffee, we trade bites of the treats, trying each one, and talk about our schedules for the upcoming week and when we can see each other. Including my staying over, which seems to be a given, and is fan-freaking-tastic.

Being with Easton is easy and fun, relaxing and exciting. I'm so glad we were friends first. It makes everything else, everything new, seem like so much *more*, amplifying it to another level.

I take one last bite of the turnover and set the remainder on the plate beside the remnants of the devoured croissant, scone, and donut.

"Wait." Easton brushes his thumb over my lip. "You have some sugar there."

I chase his flavor with a swipe of my tongue. "Must be because you're so sweet."

"Kade..." Rolling his eyes, he laughs. The smile lights up his entire face. And in this one moment, everything I love about him hits me all at once in a jolt as powerful as a dozen lightning storms.

My heart swelling with so many good feelings, I lay my hand on his warm thigh. "You look happy, East."

He beams a smile at me that rivals the sun. "I am happy. Coffee, pastries, and Kade. What more could I ask for?"

I'm melted by those words, that sparkling gaze, and how his hand curls into mine solid and strong. "How about doing this every day, for forever?"

The question hangs in the air for a second, then two, and I quiver with the blushing worry that I've asked for too much, too soon.

Easton pushes the tray aside and swings a leg over my lap, straddling me. Hands sliding around my shoulders, he brings our foreheads together for a moment, breathing with me, before he leans back and catches my gaze, his expression soft and open. "Forever sounds just about long enough."

I thought I knew what happiness was, but as I wrap him in my embrace, and am held secure in his arms, I realize that anything I felt before was dim compared to the overwhelming ecstasy of Easton Santiago telling me that forever sounds good to him too.

Our lips come together and the kiss feels like we're sealing a promise. And it's the best way to get started on building our forever.

We hope you enjoyed Kade and Easton's story. The best way to support indie authors is by leaving a review on a retailer's site, Goodreads, or your social media platforms. We appreciate your support!

Sign up for Susan and Chantal's reader newsletter: https://www.shelleyandmer.com/newsletter

If you enjoyed *Spiral*, keep reading for more about the other books in the Love & Rugby series.

Spark

Spending his fortieth birthday in a club filled with twenty-somethings and members of his brother's rugby team isn't Finlay Davidson's idea of fun, but falling into the arms of a sexy stranger who looks as out of place as Finlay feels, entices him to stay. For a decade, he's partnered with his siblings, focused on building a successful family business and ensuring the well-being of his employees. Romance hasn't been a priority, but meeting the man, who moonlights as a bouncer and is one of his brother's teammates, shifts his world and ignites his desire for more.

For the past year and a half, Mateo Rossi Ayala's life has revolved around working two jobs, bouncing on weekends and doing home remodels during the week. His only respite is the weekly rugby games and practices with teammates who have become like family. Meeting Finlay, his rugby teammate's brother, is a spark of light in a hectic life consumed by commitments and responsibilities, strong enough for Mateo to believe that the unattainable is possible.

The intensity of their immediate connection outweighs Finlay's hesitation over dating someone who plays a dangerous sport, and makes Mateo determined to fit their relationship into his life without dropping any balls. When their worlds turn upside down, Finlay's fears and Mateo's worst nightmare collide. With their differences and doubts laid bare, can their burgeoning relationship survive the strain or will their bond be severed?

Chapter One

Finlay

"Come dance with us." Cameron, my slightly inebriated brother, bumps my shoulder with his and chugs the last of his beer. "We're celebrating."

"No." I take a swig of the lukewarm beer I've been nursing for the last hour and wonder how the hell I let my siblings talk me into going out to a club for which I am entirely too old. With Cam's rugby team.

"Aileene, tell Fin to get on the dance floor." Cameron's whining drills into my temple worse than the bass of whatever song is playing. Five years my junior and the baby, my brother is charismatic and adept at getting what he wants. So, when he doesn't get his way, he reverts back to throwing tiny tantrums.

The day is unseasonably warm for early May, and the air is pungent with sweat and alcohol. Bodies on the dance floor sway and grind. Men with men. Men with women. Women with women. There are couples and throuples, groups, and some guy who appears to be dancing by himself. Eyes closed, his head lulls from side to side as his hips keep time with the music.

I squint and look closer. He could be asleep and being bounced around by the other dancers. It's a tough call. The floor is dense with people, it's hard to separate one group from the next.

I tip my bottle toward the chaos. "That has to be a fire code violation."

"Ai-leeeeeeene..." Cam falls to his knees and grabs hold of her hand.

Our sister rolls her eyes and shoves Cam off of her. "If Finlay wants to celebrate his birthday sitting and sulking—"

"I'm not sulk—"

Aileene lasers me with a look, and I shut my mouth. Somehow her crystal blue eyes look both icy and amused. I'm not sure how she manages it, but being the only girl and wedged between Cameron and me, she learned early on how to put both of us in our places. Her eyes remain glued to mine even as she speaks to Cam, and we all know I'm the target for her jabs. "If Finlay wants to sulk, there's nothing we can do to stop him from acting like a big baby."

"Cam's the one who's acting like a baby," I shoot back, sounding very much like the infant I claim not to be.

"If I'm a baby, then you're an old geezer." Cam stabs his finger into my chest and then whirls around to face our friend Hercules, who is the only person I know from Cam's team. "Who chooses to celebrate their fortieth birthday ordering take-out and re-grouting their bathroom? You didn't even have a *cake*."

"Why do you care how I choose to spend my birthday? Maybe I wanted a quiet night. Work has been hectic—"

"Because you don't delegate." My obnoxious brother is riling himself up, poking me in the chest. At the moment, he looks so much like my adorable five-year-old niece, Olive, that all annoyance dissipates. At six-three, my younger brother is built like a water buffalo. How he managed to sire a petite, cherub-like little girl like my niece is mind-boggling.

Rather than engaging—and feeling the need for something more potent—I push back in my chair and stand. "I'm getting another drink. Anyone want anything?"

"I want you to dance." Cam crosses his arms over his chest, pouting. I swear you'd never know he was part owner of a thriving company, a marketing and creative genius, and the best father I've ever seen.

Thankfully, Aileene gets up, tugging one of his arms free. "Let's go. I'll dance with you." Cam's pout morphs into excitement. "But if a cute guy presents himself, I'm cutting you loose." Our sister pushes Cam toward the dance floor.

"I'll wrestle you and put you in a headlock for far less than a cute guy." Pinning her to him, Cam locks an arm around Aileene's shoulders and noogies her.

With her graceful, dancer-like body, our much smaller sister, scream-laughs as she elbows Cam in the stomach. "Get off me, you over-sized child."

Cam releases Aileene and points his attention to the only other member of our group who isn't dancing. "You okay while we dance, Herc?"

Sitting with his leg propped up on a chair and crutches tucked out of the way, Hercules, who was injured during a rugby game two months ago, lifts his bottle. "If Fin gets me another beer, I'll be good."

"Will do." I turn and head to the bar before Cam can start with any more of his nagging. I love the guy, but when he sets his mind on something, he's relentless, and I just don't have it in me to argue with him tonight. Which is the reason I ended up here with a bunch of Cam's friends who I've never met before.

The place is packed, and jostling my way through the crowded bar to order drinks takes an eternity. Finally able to push my way to the front, I'm accosted by how out of place I am when the perky bartender yells over the din of voices and the thumping music, "What can I get you, sir?"

Sir? She called me, sir? Grant it, she doesn't look like she can be much older than twenty, if that. But sir? I definitely need something stronger than a beer if I'm going to make it another minute in this place. "Two beers and... You know what, give me a bottle of tequila and a bunch of shot glasses."

"Lemons and salt?" The bartender pops the caps from two bottles.

"Sure."

Tequila tucked under my arm, the beers in one hand and half a dozen shot glasses in the other, I begin the trek back to our table on the opposite end of the club. "Excuse me. Pardon me." It doesn't matter how loud I say the words, the Saturday night crowd of twenty-somethings is oblivious.

I am too old for this.

Dodging an elbow to the ribs, I scoot to the left, and before I know what's happening, I trip. Legs intertwine with legs. A slurred, "Yo, dude." Radiating pain flashes as my thigh bangs into the corner of the table. In an attempt not to drop everything I'm carrying, I over-correct, bumping into someone and lose my balance. The bottles and glasses clutched to my chest, I brace myself for the slam of my ass onto the concrete floor and know my tailbone is going to hurt like hell tomorrow.

But instead of connecting with the filthy floor, two strong hands from behind pull me to standing.

"You okay?" The baritone voice is so close, the warmth of his breath hits my perspiring neck, sending a shiver through me.

"Yeah, I'm good." When I turn to face the voice, I'm struck by rich brown eyes assessing me. His mouth curves, the corners of his eyes crinkle, and I get the feeling his assessment is more than making sure I'm okay. "Thank you."

The large hands that kept me on my feet are still planted on my hips. I glance down at them, and as if realizing he's still holding me, the dark-haired stranger drops them and steps back. "They can get a little rambunctious." He jerks his chin toward the crowd surrounding us. "Can I help you with some of that?"

"I'd appreciate it. Thanks." I hand him the shot glasses and remove the bottle of tequila from underneath my arm. As we weave through the crowd, I ask, "Do you come here often?" Because this doesn't look like the kind of place a guy like him would come to. And when I say a guy like him, I mean someone who is closer to my age than most of the people here.

His chuckle is a low rumble over the din of the crowd and music. "Aren't you a little old to be using a pickup line?"

Heat rushes from my neck to the top of my head, and I know my Scottish complexion is a shade of ruby that is unbecoming. "It wasn't... I wasn't..." Inhaling, I will the flutter in my chest to still. The man is sexy, but I honestly wasn't trying to pick him up. He's right. I am too old for that shit. Not to mention, how many long-term relationships start from meeting someone at a club? "I was curious because this doesn't seem like your kind of crowd."

The black tee that shows off a powerful, broad chest is tucked into black jeans that are molded to thighs I'd kill to have wrapped around me. His black boots look like he could kick the hell out of someone with them. All of it is out of place in a room full of people dressed in colors brighter than a preening peacock. He stands out. Not only because of his clothes but because he doesn't look like he's having a particularly good time. As is evident by the way he's constantly scanning the room, his firm mouth only softening when he returns his attention to me.

"You're right, it's not. But sometimes..." His gaze falls to my mouth, and for a moment, I'm twenty-three again when I was still excited about life and all of its possibilities. "Sometimes it's in unexpected places where we find the treasures."

I swear, I almost swoon.

Let's be clear, I am not a guy who is easily impressed or falls for false flattery. Being the CEO of a company employing hundreds of people whose livelihoods depend on me making good decisions, I can't afford to be. But with this man whose arms look like they've been chiseled from brown agate and polished to perfection, and the sincerity of his words in a setting where sincerity is as rare as a three-dollar beer, I could be swayed.

"I'm Finlay." Forgetting about the bottle I'm holding, I stick out my hand to shake his.

Amusement creases the corners of his eyes, and he taps the bottle with one of the shot glasses he's carrying. "Mateo. Nice to meet you, Finlay."

As we approach the tables Cam's group commandeered, Hercules and his crutches are gone, and all that is left of Cam and Aileene is Aileene's sweater hanging over the back of a chair. "Do you want to join me for a drink, Mateo?" The feel of his name on my lips is velvety smooth like old leather that has been worn and buffed to perfection.

Before he can answer, his attention is snatched by a scuffle on the dance floor. Dancers move to the edge of the floor as some guy in green shorts with whales all over them pushes a shorter man away from his dance partner and starts berating the young woman with the high ponytail.

"I've got to go." Setting the glasses on the table, Mateo pushes through the crowd like it's his job.

Shocked at the suddenness of his departure, I stand staring at his retreat, the condensation of the beers dripping onto my palm, the beating of my heart erratic and speedy.

And then I notice it.

STAFF, written in big, white letters, spans the expanse of the back of his black shirt.

The hopeful giddiness of moments ago crashes to the concrete floor, shattering my silly notions. Dropping into the seat next to my sister's sweater, I twist open the tequila and pour.

"What's this all about?" Aileene swirls her finger in the direction of the bottle of tequila as she scoots into a vacant chair.

I pour her a shot and she accepts the glass as she watches over my shoulder at the commotion on the dance floor.

In a gulp, I down the shot, welcoming the burn of my throat as it transforms to warmth when it hits my gut. "Nothing, just a birthday drink."

"That's it?" A small line forms between her brows, and I feel like she's assessing me the way she does lab experiments.

"That's it." I swig more tequila, hoping it will dull the stupidity hammering me for thinking that Mateo was doing anything other than his job. What a fool... Why would he be interested in someone as old as me when he can have his pick of hot young men. And women... if that's his thing.

"You sure?" Aileene sips her shot and wrinkles her nose. Ever since her twenty-first birthday, she's kept her distance from tequila. Sixteen years later, and it looks like she's not ready to forgive the drink.

The sound of whale-shorts yelling about being unfairly treated flutters over the vibration of the music. When I look up, Mateo and another staff person dressed all in black with STAFF on the back of his shirt—how I didn't notice that earlier is beyond me—are escorting the obnoxious, preppy jerk out of the club. Mouth a firm line, Mateo catches me watching. His eyes flat, they dart away before I have the chance to acknowledge the brief encounter.

I sigh and pour another shot feeling every single one of my forty years. "Yeah, I'm sure."

Smolder

♥

CAMERON DAVIDSON IS A devoted father, a marketing whiz for the company he owns with his siblings, and the captain of the over-thirty team for the inclusive rugby club he founded. His life is full, but he feels like something—someone—is missing. Exchanging messages with the new, anonymous, charming shopper who handles his groceries fills the void, but he longs to take the texts offline and into the real world. When the mystery man is revealed to be Aspen Ocean, the younger, attractive, and aggravating captain of the under-thirty team, Cam is forced to rethink their relationship and admit that there's more to his fascination with Aspen than his ever-changing hair color and kaleidoscope of tattoos.

Aspen Ocean loves being a makeup artist, his tight-knit friend group, and captaining the under-thirty rugby team. His second job as a personal shopper was only supposed to give him extra income, not potentially find him a boyfriend. He's floored when he learns the sexy single dad he's been flirting with is actually Cameron, who has been a thorn in his side for the last five years. The discovery compels him to concede there's something to the undercurrent of attraction swirling beneath their encounters on the pitch and acknowledge that he yearns to see what lies beneath the sarcasm and humor that Cam presents to the world.

The decision to spend time together and get to know one another properly allows Cam and Aspen to see each other in a new light. Beyond the attraction and chemistry, they find support and caring and a connection that deepens with each passing day. But Cam is protective about who he allows into his and his daughter's lives and especially into their hearts, and Aspen with his unique upbringing feels ill-equipped to navigate anything traditional, including a relationship that includes more than just him and Cam. Can the fire of what they've built blaze bright despite the obstacles or will it fizzle out?

Chapter One

Cam

"Hey, Cam." Kade from the under-thirty team waves as he sprints across the pitch and drops his backpack with the rest of his team's belongings. I return his wave and search for the teal locks of Aspen, the captain of the under-thirty team. At least that's what color his hair was on Saturday. With the frequency in which he changes his hair color, it could be orange today. Typically, he's one of the first ones here so we can set up and discuss the drills we're going to do with our teams, but today he's late.

"I'm bored, Daddy." Olive, my six-year-old, folds herself in half and swings from side to side, her blond pigtails centimeters from touching the grassy field.

"Why don't you help me set up the cones? And since Mr. Aspen isn't here yet, maybe you can help with the drills. Would you like that?" I check my phone in case Aspen has sent a message to the club's group chat, but there's nothing new there.

Olive jumps to standing, the sparkle in her blue eyes looks so much like my sister, Aileene, she could be her clone. "Yay!"

She holds out her hands and I give her four green cones. "Go set those at the far end of the pitch, then let everyone know we're starting warm-up drills in five minutes."

Darting across the field, pigtails flapping behind her, she stops to pull up her unicorn knee-high socks, then takes off again. I can't help but smile as I tuck my phone into my bag. Being a single dad can be tough at times, but I'm fortunate to have a supportive family, and I can afford help. I knew what I was getting into when I decided waiting for the perfect guy to have kids wasn't for me. What I wasn't prepared for was how in awe I'd be of the little person I created—with the help of a donor and a surrogate—or just how in love I'd fall.

Olive drops the cones then races to the group of guys standing around bullshitting. Arms waving animatedly in the air she says something. The guys laugh. My good friend, Mateo, lifts her to his shoulders and the teams fall into line, following her as she leads them to the middle of the pitch. A belly laugh fills the air as Teo swings her off his shoulders and onto the ground. Once she's directed everyone on where they should stand, she calls, "We're ready, Daddy."

I jog over. "Good job, Olive. These guys are a handful."

Olive whisper-yells over the good-natured objections of the nearly thirty men who have become my second family over the years, "It's better not to say that in front of them. It could hurt their feelings."

"You're right." I glance up at the guys, all of them as enamored with my girl as I am. "Sorry. I'll do better. Now, what should we start with?"

"Samson stretch!" Olive jumps up and down as the rest of us groan. Fingers laced together, she raises her arms over her head as she steps her left leg out in front of her far enough to bend her right knee to the ground. When she walks her right leg to her left her arms come down. "Start with ten forward, then backward. Ready... Go!"

I swear I stand a little taller when I witness the way my daughter commands a bunch of men three times her size but still retains her sweet nature. We follow Olive's lead through the warm-ups, and we are almost finished when a frazzled-looking Aspen hurries toward us.

Long, lean legs cut across the pitch, tattoos decorate his left arm and more peek out from under the hem of his shorts as he dashes to join us. A sheen of perspiration dots his forehead, and the early evening sun bounces off the fine hoop of silver hugging his ear.

Ten years my junior, Aspen is agile and has impressive footwork on the pitch. He's committed to his team, which is why they voted him captain, but he's the grumpiest dude I've ever met. Okay, that may be overstating it. The only person he seems to be grumpy with is me. The guy is so damn serious. We're here to play a game we all enjoy and have fun. It's not like we're the All Blacks fighting to keep our number one world ranking. We're a recreational rugby club in Philly.

"Nice of you to show up." Hands on my hips I give him a saccharine smile. There may be a tiny part of me that enjoys getting him riled up. And it has nothing to do with the way his blue eyes spark or how he chews on his bottom lip when he's trying to maintain his composure. I gesture to Olive. "Olive filled in for you."

He narrows his sparking eyes at me, but his features soften when he looks at my daughter, and I swear my chest sputters. Bending, so he's eye level, he holds up his hand and Olive gives him a high-five. "Thank you, Olive. That was very nice of you."

"You're welcome." She glances at his teal hair. "The next time you dye your hair, can you dye it purple?"

Great, now I have to deal with a wonky gut in addition to a sputtering chest when the expression on his face transforms to one of absolute glee. "Of course, I will. Will you be at the game on Saturday?"

Olive looks at me. "Will I, Daddy?"

"I think Hercules plans on being there." Our manny, Herc, played until he was injured last year. Typically, he watches Olive on Wednesday nights and brings her to the games on Saturdays, but tonight his study group is meeting to review material for a big test in his Advanced Child Development class.

Aspen pats Olive's head as he stands. "Then I'll make sure I have purple hair for you."

Olive beams. "I'm going to draw a picture of you with purple hair, right now."

"I can't wait to see it." The curve of his mouth is spellbinding, and for a fraction of a second, I wonder what his lips taste like.

Olive wrapping her arms around my legs pulls me from the baffling thought, and I hug her back. "Make sure you stay where I can see you."

"I will."

A piece of my heart follows her as she skips to the sideline. When I turn my attention back to Aspen, he's studying me, and the strain of his pinched lips chafes. My toes curl in my cleats, and I hold tight to my grin as a cloud of disappointment hovers over me. I don't know what I'm disappointed about, I'm usually on this side of his scowls. "I thought we'd do mauling drills today. We won't have time for much more than that."

"Fine." His curt reply is as prickly as falling into a field of thistles, and just as painful.

"Look," I swing around so I'm standing directly in front of him and thrust a tackling shield at him. "If you want to do something else, say it. You weren't here. No text to tell me you were running late, no call, nothing. So, I had to plan the practice without your input. Next time, some communication would be nice." My chest heaves with pent-up frustration. I do not need someone with a stick up his ass to ruin my or anyone else's Wednesday night. This is supposed to be *fun*.

His thick eyelashes flutter, and I'm struck by how long they are. I remember overhearing him tell some asshole who was trying to pick him up when a bunch of us went out for beers after our games, that he had the same mutation as Elizabeth Taylor, leaving him with a double row of lashes.

"I apologize." The smoky smoothness of his voice grates on my nerves. How someone can sound both contrite and condescending with only two words is as perplexing as the torturous thrill the tinted-glass tone triggers low in my spine and is one more reason this guy bugs the hell out of me. "My last appointment at the salon was late. And when her grandmother asked if I would do her makeup too, I couldn't tell her, no."

I deflate. "Oh... No, I guess not. I can never refuse my gran anything."

We stand there staring at each other. I'm not sure where my outburst came from, but it makes me itchy and unsettled.

"Are you two done bickering?" Owen, a physical therapist who plays on my team, tosses a ball to Mateo, and the two of them share some kind of look.

Aspen hands the tackling shield to Easton, a player on his team who also happens to be one of the scientists at my company. "Let's start with bag-then-rip with two players. Then we'll move to four players." He glances at me. "You okay with that?"

"Yep." I pop the *P* and avoid eye contact.

"It's like listening to my parents," Easton mumbles before heading to the cones.

Ignoring the comment and the plethora of feelings churning in my gut, I bump Aspen in the ass with my tackling shield. "Race ya." I take off, pumping my legs, the cool evening air kissing my cheeks as the sun slowly dips in the sky. Looking over my shoulder, I halt. Aspen is jogging—not racing—over to where his team is waiting. "Party pooper," I yell.

He signals that he hears me then starts talking to his team.

The guy is so annoying.

Due to shorter days and cooler temperatures our autumn practices are only an hour. Although, this year I may be able to get us time at the Phield House on one of their indoor fields. I've put off bringing it up because it's an added cost and I don't want the club to be a burden to anyone.

Still breathing heavily from the workout, Mateo, Owen, and I sprint to our things–because some people know how to loosen up at practice, unlike others. As soon as I reach the bleachers, Olive runs and jumps into my arms. Squeezing her to me, I plant a kiss on her cheek. "Pee-ew, Daddy, you stink like sweat."

"That's because I'm sweaty." I put my wiggling girl down. "Go pick up all your markers and crayons. We've got to get a move on so we can get you bathed and into bed."

"Okay, but first I want to give Mr. Aspen the picture I made for him." She waves a paper in the air as she sprints to where Aspen, Easton, and Kade are chatting.

Easton and Kade stand beside each other, their shoulders and arms touching, fingers laced together. It's been a little over a year since they got together, but they still act like not touching each other when they're together is unbearable. It's sweet, and I'm happy to count them as one of my success stories.

Almost immediately, and without my consent, my attention lasers on Aspen. Crouching to talk to Olive, his shorts ride up his muscular legs, showing off more of his tattoos. He has the body of a long-distance runner, every muscle, sleek and defined.

"You should ask him out." Mateo hands me Olive's backpack and the beach towel she was sitting on. "I think I got everything."

"Thanks."

"I'm serious, Cam. Ask him out. It doesn't have to be anything major, coffee, a beer, pie, anything." Mateo peers at me with the intensity he usually saves for on-field action.

Baffled, I gape at my teammate. In the five years we've known each other, he's never, *never* made such a ridiculous suggestion. "What are you talking about?"

"Dude." He juts his chin toward Aspen. "You and Aspen."

I throw my head back and laugh so loudly a dog walking with his people barks. "Oh my god." Clutching my middle, I bend over. "Oh my god." I reach up and slap Mateo on the back. Just because he's found love with my brother, Finlay, doesn't mean we all need to be partnered up. "Wait until I tell Fin you've lost your mind."

Mateo stifles his amusement and shakes his head. "Whatever. But maybe if you two sat down and had an actual conversation instead of picking at each other, you'd find—"

"Thanks, Teo. I needed a good laugh." Grabbing my pack, I fish out my phone from the front pocket and note the time. "Shit. Do you mind rounding up the equipment, and I'll get it from you tomorrow? I've got to get moving if I want to make sure Olive gets to bed at a decent hour."

"Will do." Mateo's agreement is automatic as he wipes a towel over his face, arms, and neck, removing sweat, grass stains, and streaks of dirt.

"Thanks, man." We do a quick hug/backslap. Slinging both mine and Olive's backpacks over my shoulder, I cup my hands to my mouth. "Time to go, Olive Oil." She throws her arms around Aspen's shoulders before racing toward me. I hold out my hand and she catches it. "You ready, kiddo?"

"Can we stop at the store and get bananas? Hercules ate the last one today."

There is no speedy in-and-out at the grocery store with this kid. Once, we did a quick milk run; forty-five minutes and four bags later we walked out with everything but the milk. "We don't have time tonight, but I'll put an order in with GroceryGazelle for tomorrow. That way you'll have bananas when you get home from school. Deal?"

She gives her head an exaggerated nod. "Deal."

As the evening sky captures the last fading light, I walk hand-in-hand with my girl, content with the life I've created, and ignore the prickling along my skull that something is missing.

Shine

♥

HERCULES HOFFMAN HAS SPENT the last few years starting over, in a new job, new living situation, going back to college, and in a new role as manager of the inclusive rugby club he used to play for. His friendships are solid but with his life in transition, he doesn't believe he has a lot to offer someone until the goals he's working towards are achieved. From their first meeting on the pitch, Hercules sees Apollo as out of his reach, but the gentle giant is never far from his thoughts.

Zoologist Apollo Leos finds animals easier to understand than people. Joining the rec league rugby club pushed him out of his comfort zone and gave him a supportive friend group for the first time in his life. Slowly shedding the shields he developed to protect himself from the harshness of the world, he's gaining confidence and the ability to relax and trust. Except when it comes to his attraction to Hercules. He's never dated before and feels his inexperience will be seen as a hindrance to a relationship. Not knowing how Hercules will react to that information freezes him from making the first move.

After their matchmaking friends scheme to get them together, Hercules and Apollo take a tentative step that quickly falls into a heady rush of firsts. Kisses, dates, sharing pieces of themselves, they form a bond based on support and trust that opens up their worlds. As Hercules wars with doubts about himself and Apollo navigates the unfamiliar territory of a romantic relationship, their summer romance is tested by Hercules's belief that people don't stick around and Apollo's worry about what will happen when he trusts someone with his heart.

Chapter One

Hercules

The air is thick with humidity, making my shirt stick to my torso and my shorts suction to my thighs. Though it is only mid-June, we're experiencing the fourth day of a heatwave with no end in sight.

Taking the hair tie from my wrist, I gather my hair and twist it to the middle of my head, freeing my neck of the stifling blanket. Conversations and laughter from my friends drift around me. Watching a few of them toss around a football, I drag my chair closer to one of the many misters peppering the patio under the pergola and enjoy a moment of stillness after a morning spent helping with preparations.

When Cam decided two weeks ago to have a cookout celebrating the end of school for Olive and me, it seemed like a good idea. Now, I fear I'll die of a heat stroke *and* have swamp ass.

"Watch the coop," Cameron Davidson, my friend, boss, and the heart and soul behind the rugby rec club I played in until my injury, calls from his perch at the grill to Owen and Greer who are diving for the football across the grass.

We all know the kind of damage rugby players can do. Heck, I have a four-inch scar on my leg as proof. The ruffled apron Cam is sporting looks like something a fifties-era housewife would wear rather than the blond, water buffalo of a man twirling the spatula on his finger to get a laugh out of his little girl.

Olive, Cam's daughter, and my charge, claps her hands. "Let me try, Daddy."

Before Cam gives Olive the spatula, he points it at Greer. "You break the coop; the chickens are spending the night with you until you fix it."

"Hey, where are Fin and Mateo?" Greer tosses the football back to Owen, and they move away from the coop.

"Fin took Mateo on a romantic weekend getaway." Cam watches Olive set the spatula spinning. His brother called last night while he and Teo, his boyfriend who also plays in the rugby league, were on their way to the airport.

The football arcs through the air. Greer hoots his laughter as the ball twirls five feet to the left of him, inches from hitting the roof of the chicken coop. "Dude, maybe if you could throw the ball..."

Owen lifts his hands, palms up. "I'm used to a rugby ball."

"Give it up, Owen. Come play corn hole with us." Aspen, Cam's boyfriend, waves Owen over. "We'll play teams."

From behind my sunglasses, I let my gaze drift to the tall man at the far end of the corn hole game. His long, wavy hair is up in its usual man bun, and his grin, which is usually shy and apprehensive, is shining as bright as the mid-day sun and is just as hot. Apollo Leos joined the rec rugby team a little over a year ago, but I first noticed him when he brought several zoo animals to Olive's sixth birthday party last year. His large frame and gentle, almost timid manner were enough to hook me instantly.

Olive runs to Aspen. "Can I be on your team?"

Aspen takes her hand. "Of course you can."

Seeing how Cam, Aspen, and Olive are becoming a unit, I can't help but be thrilled, and a wee bit envious, of my friends and the life they're creating. I figured by thirty-three, I'd have my shit together. Instead, I'm a live-in manny who just completed the first year of my Master's in Early Childhood Education. Again, my focus lands on the sexy zoologist. Maybe one day I'll have enough to offer to keep someone like him around.

Owen jogs to Apollo, and the two shake hands, slapping each other on the back in a half-hug.

"What about me?" Greer follows Owen, and before I know it, I'm out of my chair. Greer is a nice guy, but he's forever on the hunt for the next love of his life. The need to shelter Apollo from any distress he might experience if he gets involved with Greer propels me forward.

"You play with Olive and me." At Aspen's directive, Greer changes directions, high-fiving Olive when he reaches the duo.

Plopping back into my seat, I feel eyes on me. I don't have to look to know whose they are, but I do anyway to find Cam's mouth turned skyward and his scheming eyes dancing. Shit. For a year, I've been able to keep my interest in Apollo to myself. But the look on Cam's face is the equivalent of being caught with my hand in the cookie jar. He knows...

My attention is torn from my friend when Olive says, "But then the teams will be uneven. Mr. Apollo and Mr. Owen need a third person."

"Herc will play." Beaming, Cam displays zero shame in his meddling. Once he gets an idea in his head that two people should be together, he feels it's his duty to play matchmaker. I glare at him. "What? You look like you want to play? Plus," He gestures to his sister, her boyfriend, and a few other guys from the team who are in deep conversation and downing cool drinks by the misters. "Everyone else is otherwise engaged."

"Yay!" Olive runs over and tugs on my hand before I can flip off her father—which I would never do in front of her but have no qualms about doing when she's not looking. "C'mon Hercules, your team needs you."

Ignoring Aspen's questioning eyebrow, I follow Olive and her bouncing braids. The instant the sun hits the top of my head, perspiration gathers at my hairline, but when I glimpse a strip of dark blond fur on firm abs trailing into Apollo's low-slung shorts, I'm set aflame.

Owen pats my back. "Welcome to the team, man."

Having lost my voice because... abs and skin that are wet-dream worthy, I wet my lips and nod.

Apollo drops the hem of the shirt he was using to wipe his face and smiles. Gone is the carefree expression, a shy, reserved grin taking its place. "Hi, Hercules."

"Hey." Rubbing the back of my neck, I break eye contact. The last thing I want is for Apollo, or anyone for that matter, to see the crush of disappointment that tackles me by the change in his demeanor.

"Ready?" Aspen calls. "First team to ten wins."

"We're gonna win. We're gonna win." With Olive standing on his feet and screeching her laughter, Greer does the Meringue around their board.

Apollo picks up a red bean bag, tosses it in the air then catches it in his big hand. At over six-and-a-half feet tall, his build is powerful, but he's not bulky like Cam. His hands are large, his fingers are long and graceful looking, and my cock strains with want to be held by them. "Do we get extra points for hitting the hole with obstructions?"

"Move out of the way so we can get started. The burgers are going to be ready soon." Aspen tugs on Greer's shirt, and he dances Olive behind the board.

Apollo hands the bean bag to Owen. "You first." He steps back. His arm grazes mine, inducing a frantic rush of flutters in my chest. "I knew Aspen would reel Greer in." He watches Owen launch the bean bag. Barely missing Greer's head, it lands within inches of the koi pond. The twitching of Apollo's lips combined with the pressure of his arm still pressed to mine makes the moment seem intimate.

"Jeez, O, do you even know how to aim?" Greer taunts as he jogs to pick up the bag.

"My turn!" Olive catches the blue bean bag Aspen tosses her.

Owen laughs and turns to us. "I love messing with Greer."

"And Greer loves messing with everyone," I grunt.

Owen snaps back his head, his eyes wide with disbelief because that came out way more catty than I intended. "*Me-ow.* Who pissed on your pillow this morning?"

I pinch the bridge of my nose. "I didn't mean it like that. Must be the heat."

"Would you like me to get you some water?" Squeezing my shoulder, Apollo is so sincere; it's all I can do to keep my hands to myself when wrapping my arms around his middle and burrowing my nose in his neck is all I can think of.

Stepping out of his reach, I move until his arm falls to his side. "I'm good. Thanks."

His piercing eyes dart over my face, and I'm stunned by how open and raw they are before he lowers his head and gives a gentle nod. When he looks up again, I question whether what I saw was real or what I wanted to see. The latter being more likely since the eyes looking at me now, while still piercing, are concealed, private.

Scooping up the bean bags, I hand them to Apollo. "You're up."

"Thanks." He takes careful aim and lobs the bag in an underhand throw. It hits the board near the top, slides down, and falls through the hole.

"Nice!" Owen high-fives Apollo. When Apollo looks at me, I give him a nod, wishing I could do more.

One does not often think of corn hole as a cut-throat game. However, our crew changes that notion. Aspen charges and tackles me to keep from tying the game, and Owen tells so many corny jokes Olive can hardly breathe, let alone toss the bag from laughing so hard.

As our game descends further into a good-natured melee of chaos, we're saved by Cam. "Who wants cheese?"

"Me, please." Olive raises her hand, and the five of us follow, raising our hands too.

"Olive, let's go wash up quickly before we eat." I bend at my knees, and she hops on my back.

"Can I come?" Looking at the ground, Apollo walks alongside us, his question asked as if he's afraid to intrude.

His arm brushes mine and ignites a craving to feel more than that tiny touch. "Sure."

"Then I can show you my axolotl. Her name is Herman." Over my shoulder, Olive points to the door, like she's leading an expedition.

Lips twitching again, he glances at me, stirring my insides and making me... want. But wanting doesn't do any good if one doesn't have something to give in return.

"Why did you name her Herman?" Though it's clear he's amused by Olive's name selection, his question is asked with genuine curiosity and respect. Too often, adults don't demonstrate the kind of respect kids deserve and end up stifling or making children feel silly for things they say or the choices they make. That Apollo seems to understand his, ups his attractiveness factor and ramps up my crush on the man.

"She looks like a Herman." Reaching the house, I squat, and Olive slides off.

"Most axolotls do." He hooks his sunglasses into his shirt collar.

Cocking her head to the side, Olive taps her chin, looking every bit like Cam's kid. "You're right."

"Although it's known as a walking fish, the axolotl is actually an amphibian. A salamander." Apollo opens the sliding glass door. The cool air smacking us in the faces is a bigger relief than when I was laid off from my soul-sucking job last year.

"I guess a zoologist would know a few things about animals." Following the two of them into the kitchen, I pull out the stool for Olive and place it at the sink. Then, like the well-oiled machine we are, she hops up to wash her hands.

"Hercules is taking me to the zoo tomorrow. Right, Herc?" Olive shakes her hands, scattering water drops on the sink and counter.

I hand her a towel. "I am."

"Really?" Apollo's face lights up. "You two should stop by and see me. I'm doing a small group presentation on giraffes." He folds his large body in half and whispers into Olive's ear, "And everyone there will get to hand-feed Stella, Abigail, and Bea."

Olive takes Apollo's cheeks in her hands, and with the utmost seriousness, says, "I. Love. Giraffes."

Delighted, he places his hands over hers but doesn't remove them from his face. "I know. And I think our giraffes do too. They like that you visit them so much."

"I'm going to tell Daddy."

I stop her before she rushes out the door. "What do you say to Mr. Apollo?"

"Thank you!" She bolts, leaving the door wide open.

Apollo chuckles and closes it. "Someone's excited."

"You didn't have to do that." I wash my hands and splash water over my face and neck. He passes me a hand towel, and I dry off. "If it's going to be a hassle, we can do it some other time."

Looking at the polished marble floor, he shakes his head. "It's no problem. There's a group of eight, and we have ten spots. The presentation is at eleven, so if you can get there by ten-thirty, that would be great."

Curious as to why Apollo is back to looking at the floor, I set the towel on the island. "Okay."

Lifting his eyes, he studies me, and there's something about his intensity that makes me feel stripped naked. "Okay?"

"Yeah. Thanks." Clearing my throat, I jut my chin toward the door. "I better check to see if Cam needs help. See you out there."

He lifts a long-fingered hand, and I scurry out the door, the heat of outside not near as intense as the heat I feel when I'm close to Apollo. Before I can claim my breath,

Cam hands me a plate with a burger, chips, and fruit salad on it. "Where's Apollo?"

"Washing up." I take the plate and look for a quiet corner to sit and regroup. Since first meeting Apollo, I've interacted with him, but I've made a point of limiting the interactions. Being around him for any length of time tips my world, leaving me feeling wonky and a little woozy.

"He just made Olive's year." He lowers his voice. "So, how long have you had a thing for him?"

"I don't—"

Cam tips his chin to his chest, his face stern and unyielding, telling me without saying a word that I better not even try to deny what we both know to be true.

"Fine. For a while." That my huffy-whine sounds like Olive when she's been caught fudging the truth doesn't escape me, nor does it Cam if his knowing smirk is any indication.

"And..." He steals a cantaloupe ball from my plate and pops it into his mouth.

"And I'm not in a place to pursue anything with anyone. So please, *please* do not start with your matchmaking." No, I am not above begging. Cam is all about making people happy, or rather, what *he* thinks will make them happy. Grant it, he's usually correct, but I'm choosing not to acknowledge that now.

Staring at me, he nods. "If that's what you want."

I let out a long relieved sigh. "It is. Thank you."

Behind me, the sliding glass door opens and closes, and not knowing what to expect with Cam, I tense. Cam's expression morphs from concerned friend to friendly party host. He lifts the plate in his hand. "I made a plate for you."

"Thanks." Apollo takes the plate and looks between Cam and me. "Am I interrupting something?"

Cam pats Apollo on the back. "Nope. I was just talking to Herc about inviting everyone down to the beach house the week of the Fourth of July."

My stomach pitches and my heart accelerates as I narrow my eyes at my so-called friend.

"Cool." Apollo bites into a cookie while I stand frozen, glowering at Cameron. "Oh my god. Who made these cookies?"

Cam points to me. "Herc is a great cook, but baking is his specialty."

Apollo shoves the rest of the lemon cookie in his mouth, his eyes fluttering shut as he hums, and I wonder if he looks the same when he comes.

My dick hardens, and... I'm getting a chubby watching a guy eat a cookie. This is not good.

After the longest thirty seconds of my life, Apollo finishes his pornographic food tasting. "I won't be able to take off the whole week, but I can swing the weekend. I might be able to come down early Friday."

"Excellent." Cam pats Apollo's back again. "I'll send out a group email with details tomorrow. Okay," he looks around the backyard. "I'm going to check on everyone. You two good?" Smug is the only word to describe the annoying man. We will have words later.

Apollo holds up his burger. "I'm good. Thanks."

"I'll leave you two to it then." Cam nods and has the nerve to wink at me before strolling off.

Oh, we are *definitely* having words later.

Tugging on the ends of his hair, Apollo nods toward a few open chairs by Greer, Aspen, and Owen. "Want to sit?"

"Sure." I follow a step behind, casting my gaze on everything but him. Sitting between Owen and Apollo, I balance my plate on my thigh.

The breeze shifts and carries his intoxicating scent to me. His voice, as he speaks to Aspen, caresses my ears like a sexy ballad. Apollo bites into the burger and the blissed-out pleasure overtaking his features has my cock perking up yet again.

If sitting beside him is this hard, how will spending the weekend with him be?

I'm going to kill Cam.

Surprise

♥

Greer Fox is a teacher, an actor, and a hopeless romantic. He has a life he adores but longs to find a love like his friends have with their partners. Despite getting bruised, he keeps his heart open. Catching feelings for Owen Kim, his secret hookup buddy from his rugby club, surprises Greer, but he's open to exploring whatever might come from a relationship with Owen.

Physical therapist Owen Kim's life has revolved around building and expanding his practice. In his black and white world, Greer provides the color. What started out as fun and casual has now opened his eyes to what he's been missing, and Greer is the catalyst to exploring what he hasn't let himself have in years.

A new year's eve spent dancing and kissing with their mutual crush, meteorologist Storm Breen, gives the trio a taste of what can happen when desires are explored and the knowledge that they want more of what they can bring to each other.

Fitting each other into their lives is almost seamless and the trio clicks together like nothing else they've ever experienced. Neither Greer nor Storm have been in a relationship with more than one person before, and Owen fears the reason his last triad ended could repeat itself. Their deepening bond brings vulnerabilities to light, and sharing secrets, needs, and feelings isn't easy for three men who have very good reasons for keeping their defenses in place, even though those walls have the power to tear them apart.

Chapter One

Greer

Laughter, music, and conversations flow around me, mixing with the scents of cinnamon and pine the aromas of food drifting from a heavily laden table. Twinkling lights adorning nearly every surface in the room, from the windows, to the tables, and the massive holiday tree.

Standing by the crackling fireplace, I take a look around the home of my best friend's boyfriend. Our friends and teammates are spread throughout the living room, family room, and kitchen, decked out for our rugby club's annual holiday party in sweaters ranging from whimsical to classic to gaudy. Today may only be December eleventh, but the hint of expectation and anticipation is already in the air.

This evening is a welcome respite from the stress of teaching the basics of acting to college kids who are not into actually doing the work this semester and from a time of year that is especially hard for me. I've been scanning the party for a certain someone who could provide me with a certain type of sexy distraction, but he has yet to arrive.

"Greer, you look like you need a cocktail." Aspen comes up to me, his hair the color of cranberries, sparkling dark green liner highlighting his eyes, and a red and green sweater with a large white reindeer across the front completing his festive look. What grabs me most is the sheer happiness glowing through his features. We've been best friends for four years and I've never seen him as content as he is with Cam.

"I do." Pushing my less than happy thoughts away, I sling my arm over his shoulder and steer him to a table covered with bottles of wines and liquors. "I was thinking about a white chocolate peppermint martini. Want one?"

"I do." He grabs glasses for us and I get to work shaking and mixing. Aspen brushes his hand over the shoulder of my sweater. "This is nice. No one else here has one that actually lights up."

I glance at the blinking rainbow of lights adorning the snowmen on my torso. "I'm regretting not buying the matching elf hat. Though, I guess I could always wind a strand of lights around my head."

Snickering, he bumps his shoulder into mine. "That, or borrow the headband with reindeer antlers that Cam brought home for the dog. Although, I haven't seen it in a few days."

"I'll keep an eye out for it." I pour the concoction and then add small candy canes to both drinks as a finishing touch. Before Aspen can reach for a glass, I lift one for him and adopt the formal toned British accent I used for an audition I went to last month. "Here you are, sir. One white chocolate peppermint martini."

Lips twitching, Aspen takes hold of the glass. "I think you would have made an excellent butler. I'm sorry you didn't get that role."

Grinning, I drop the accent. "Worked out for the best. Not getting the role means more time to work on the screenplay I abandoned at the start of the semester. Plus, I have a lot of work to do for the community theater program's fundraiser coming up in January."

"I blocked out my schedule for that entire day, so I'll be available to help out with makeup and hair." He waits for me to raise my glass. "Cheers."

"Cheers." I take a sip of chocolate and mint that tastes like the holidays.

Glass to his lips, Aspen hums his approval of the drink. "I told Cam I'd get him a drink too. I think he'd like this."

I scan the room for Aspen's hulking boyfriend, but he's not in here. "There should be enough left in the shaker for one more drink."

Aspen sets out a new glass and holds it steady as I pour, then hugs me, quick and hard. "I'm really happy you'll be here celebrating Christmas with us."

"I am, too." Our relationship has evolved since he and Cam got together and the changes haven't been easy. I joke that I and the rest of our core squad—Easton, Kade, and Apollo—share Aspen with Cam, but it's true.

Cam enters the room with Easton and Kade. The trio are laughing and give us a wave, but Cam gets waylaid by two new arrivals. Neither of whom are the one man I'm wanting to walk through the door and maybe that's for the best.

Yes, it's probably for the best.

Aspen lifts his glass and Cam's. "I'd better take this to him. Those guys will keep talking and Cam won't get a break."

"Go ahead."

"Thanks for the drinks," he calls over his shoulder. Once Cam's gaze lands on Aspen, it transforms from jovial to smitten. My heart aches. To find a love like that...

Easton and Kade head my way. They're such an in sync couple, it's almost like a dance the way they move and interact, their awareness of each other obvious in every moment.

Kade grins at me. "Cam was showing us the new decorations he added to the backyard, glittering, light-up chickens wearing Santa hats."

Easton pulls me in for a quick hug. "Did you get anything to eat yet? We didn't."

"No." I take a sip of my drink and eye the food tables. "I don't know if I want to go with the sliders, the mac and cheese, or those chicken wraps."

"I'm starting with desserts." Kade grabs three plates and passes two to Easton and me. "East, you can get the other stuff for us."

As Easton and I move down the buffet of finger foods, Kade loads up on a pile of different types of cookies. We claim a small table by a window wreathed in white lights with pine branches and poinsettias. I eat, watching Easton and Kade share the foods and treats they collected. Of all of the couples in our friend group, they've been together the longest.

"Do you have room for two more?" Apollo approaches us with his boyfriend of a few months, Hercules, both holding plates piled high. All of us had a hand in getting them together and are proud of our matchmaking efforts.

I slide over my chair to make room, bumping into Kade in the process. "Sure."

"Just grab one chair. I'll sit with Kade." Easton vacates his chair and settles half on Kade's lap and half on the wide window sill.

Apollo takes the open seat and Herc brings another chair over. I try to pay attention to talk of Herc's classes, the animals under Apollo's care at the zoo, the jobs Kade's recent motorcycle repair job, and the new product Easton is developing at the condom company, which is owned by Cam and his siblings, but the pesky knowledge that I'm flanked by couples and have Cam and Aspen in easy view keeps popping into my head.

Being the only single one in our core group is hard sometimes, but especially since I caught feelings for Owen Kim. Member of the over-thirty team, physical therapist, and my secret, occasional hookup partner since July.

The doorbell chimes, layering over the soft sleigh bells of the song emanating from hidden speakers. I glance toward the entryway, and my pulse thrums harder at the figure entering the room.

Owen looks amazing in a bright blue sweater that compliments his dark hair, brown eyes, and sepia-toned skin. From across the room, he meets my gaze and gives me a nod.

With a weak smile, I wave. I haven't seen him since our club's end of season party in November. Catching feelings isn't good. We said we were only having fun, and I promised Aspen I wouldn't date anyone in the club.

In the window's reflection, I catch myself fidgeting with my ring. Made from the metals of my parents' melted down wedding bands, I play with it when needing comfort. Unfortunately for me, or fortunately depending on the situation, my friends are all aware of that tell. Not wanting questions, I shove my hand under the table and out of sight.

Laughter erupts from my table mates. I snap my attention back to them, and the tail end of a story Kade is telling. I chuckle too, but have no idea of the premise. Their voices became a buzz when Owen walked in.

I'm not going to sit here, staring and wanting. Pushing my chair back, I grab my empty plate and glass. "Anyone want a refill on anything?"

A chorus of "no's" answers me.

The drinks table is thankfully free of people. In my peripheral vision, Owen circulates through the room. Nerves tightening my stomach, I grab the vanilla vodka, peppermint schnapps, and white chocolate liqueur so I can put together another white chocolate peppermint martini. All I need to do is play calm and cool and unaffected for another hour or so, and then I can go home and pretend I'm not having a romantic crisis.

"Greer." Owen's voice is like a caress.

I manage to give him the easy, friendly smile I save for my students. "Hey. Want a drink?"

He usually orders Scotch at post-game gatherings, but stops me with a hand to my forearm when I reach for the bottle of his preferred brand. "I'll try whatever you're making."

That little touch singes me. I add in more of the alcohol to make enough for two drinks. "I like your sweater. Look good on you."

He glances at the snowflakes woven into the blue knit like he doesn't see anything special about the way it hugs his fit body then gives my shirt a thorough study that has me sucking in a breath. The corners of his mouth curl up. "Thanks. Yours could guide Santa's sleigh."

I huff a sigh, but can't keep a straight face or feign indignation. "The lights are *not* that bright."

"I wish I hadn't left my sunglasses in the car."

We smile at each other and my stomach does a little flip flop. He's so close to me, I could touch him. I really want to touch him. My fingers itch to run along his sweater and dive into his hair. Instead, I press the drink into his hand. "What are you doing for your birthday? I've never known an Xmas Day baby before. You're the first."

Brows lifting, he huffs out a laugh and takes a step back. "How'd you know when my birthday is?"

"I saw it on the spreadsheet Hercules put together with all of the club members' info last season when looking up the dates guys had marked they'd be unavailable to play." We all have access to the spreadsheet. I wonder if he's ever checked it out. "So, what's the plan? A party? Dinner out somewhere?"

He shrugs. "No plans other than seeing my family for Christmas dinner. People don't often remember my birthday. It gets lost in the busyness of the holiday."

That's sad. Birthdays should be big celebrations. Making a mental note to get whatever teammates I can to at least sign a card for him, I take a sip of the minty chocolate drink. "How has work been? When I had dinner here last week, Cam mentioned you've been busy."

Owen gives the candy cane stirrer in his drink an amused glance. "Yeah, I've been focused on expanding the practice. Putting in a lot of hours."

"He mentioned you weren't fun anymore." I stir the candy cane through my drink.

He copies my action, moving the striped white and red stick around his glass. "Did he, now?"

"Yep. Something about you missing weekly workouts with him and the guys."

"Now that things are paying off at work, I can free up more time." Mischievous glee overtaking his features, he brings the candy cane to his lips and sucks it into his mouth. Knowing what those lips feel like against my own and against my skin, I hold back a moan. "So, since I plan most of those workouts, he's going to regret his comment."

"Uh oh," I tease. "That sounds ominous."

"Leg day is going to suck for him."

"Are you going to tell him it's thanks to me?"

He tilts his head to the side, considering me. "What's my silence worth to you?"

My thoughts turn steamy. Sexy. I eliminate the space between us and lower my voice to a whisper. "I'm already making you one of my kick ass cocktails. Or if you wanted something more... intimate... How about my lips wrapped around your dick?"

He licks his lips, his eyes going heavy lidded. "I do like your cock and your tail. And your mouth on my dick."

My pulse is skittering, my breath coming faster, and my cock is filling. "Is that a yes?"

"Let's call it an I.O.U. and I can collect—"

"What are you two whispering about over here?" Kade's voice jolts me into Owen. My drink sloshes over the rim and drips onto my fingers.

I jump back, grabbing a napkin from the table as Easton joins Kade in our corner, my thoughts scrambling. "Work. We were talking about work."

Owen's mouth quirks and he discretely adjusts himself, shifting to hide his lower half behind the table's end. "Right. Work. I've been so busy I missed out on workouts with Cam and the guys."

"And I was telling Owen that final exams are this week. I'll be busy this coming weekend since the faculty have to submit their grades by next Monday."

His arm around Kade's waist, Easton turns to Owen. "Last year during final grading, Greer subsisted on candy bars, coffee, and so little sleep I don't know how he wasn't hallucinating."

I hold up a hand in protest. "I was not that bad."

"You were." Kade lifts a brow in challenge and I can only shrug because he's right. "The night you submitted the grades, you fell asleep at Apollo's and slept through the entire next day. Even the dogs barking didn't rouse you."

Pursing his lips, Owen makes a micro-shift toward me then stops. "That's not good. Sleep is important."

I wave away his concern. "Last year, I was filling in backstage at a show, helping out a friend of mine who lost half of his stage crew to the flu."

"Regardless, we're still checking on you this year, bud." East claps me on the back. "Aspen assigned us shifts."

The thoughtful gesture proves I have the best friends. Even when they're busy with the lives they've created with their significant others, they've still got my back. "I'll try to make your check-ins with me as entertaining as possible."

"We'd expect nothing less." Grinning, Kade raises his beer in a toast to me. "East and I ran into Wyatt and Anderson in the kitchen. They took ride shares here. I told them we'd drive them home since they're not that far from us. I think the three of you should fit in the backseat okay."

The backseat of their tiny, electric car? Anderson alone will take up half the space with his cinder block shoulders. "It'll be cozy."

"I can give Greer a ride home." Owen lays his hand on my shoulder, his voice firm and smooth. I've never been to his place. I know he lives in Fairmount, but that's all.

The touch of his hand on my shoulder is too good. Maybe those pesky feelings that have developed are more due to the orgasms we've shared and less to anything else. "Are you sure? I'm not taking you out of your way?"

"You're only about four miles from me. A twelve minute drive, fifteen max."

"Thanks."

A few of the guys from the over-thirty team are wandering over, calling for Owen. He turns to talk with them and I duck out of the way, holding my glass high as I follow Easton and Kade over to where Aspen, Wyatt, and Apollo are gathered at Cam's Steinway.

Notes of a familiar, non-holiday song fill the air, thanks to Apollo's talented hands. Wyatt drapes his arm around my shoulders with the added weight of someone feeling the effects of their alcohol intake. "We're singing. I gave Apollo a few requests from our karaoke list."

"Let's do it." I lean into my friend and the music and try not to wonder too much about what will happen once Owen and I are alone.

Outside, the air is cold and crisp. Hands tucked into my pockets, I walk beside Owen to his car. "So, now that we're alone, tell me. Was this offer a way for you to cash in that I.O.U.?"

Face lit by a street light, he leers at me. "Maybe. Unless you're not feeling it tonight."

With a shiver that I will happily pretend was caused by the cold, I hunch into my coat. "I was feeling it the moment you walked in."

His car is comfortable and warms up fast. He lets me control the radio, and I spend the ride playing DJ as we drive through the darkened streets and suburban Wynnewood turns into concrete and buildings of Philadelphia and then Queen Village, the neighborhood that's been my home since I moved to Philly five years ago.

Climbing the two-flight walk up to my studio apartment, with Owen's footsteps thudding after mine on the carpeted stairs, moments from the three previous times we've ended up back here play through my mind like snippets of sexy scenes starring us.

At the top of the landing, I dig out my keys. Owen's hands land on my shoulders, dull weights through the thick fabric of my coat. He leans into my back, his breath tickling my neck.

Managing to get the door unlocked and open without dropping my keys, I lead him into my darkened apartment. Instead of switching on the lamps, I plug in the lights on the Christmas tree. Dozens of tiny bulbs flare into glowing orbs of violet. The star at the top shines the brightest with tones of purple and blue.

"I like your tree." Owen hangs his coat over the back of a chair and toes off his shoes.

Amid the branches are blown glass balls done by a local artist and ornaments that celebrate Philly, from soft pretzels and cheesesteaks to the LOVE sculpture and Boat House Row. I slip off my coat and bend to remove my combat boots. "I do, too."

When I stand, Owen strides to me, his face mostly in shadows except for the faint brushes of light from the tree. He pulls me against his body. "You said something about your lips and my dick."

I slide my hands down his muscled torso then under his sweater to find his belt. "I did."

The hands on my shoulders glide up my neck and his thumbs graze the underside of my chin, urging my face to lift. His eyes glint with want. In the span of a breath, his mouth settles over mine, urgent and hungry. Clutching his belt, I tug myself closer, deepening the kiss, tasting and savoring, my heart beating faster and desire swirling in my blood.

His cock is hard, pressing into my hip. Mine is the same, and he has to feel the effect he has on me. He takes a step forward, his body urging me back one step, then another. The hands framing my face slide to my back and Owen changes the angle of the kiss and directs me another step backward.

Having to trust that he's not going to guide me into the path of a chair or table, I cling to that belt, the backs of my fingers brushing the hot skin of his lower torso and the edge of his boxers, and let him lead in both the kiss and the walk.

We come to a stop beside my couch. Owen raises his head. I wish I could tell what he's thinking. He grabs the hem of my sweater. "As much as I do like this shirt, it has to go."

"So I guess the lights weren't too blinding after all?" I have to release my hold of his belt so he can slide the sweater and the T-shirt I wore underneath off of me. Bare chested, my skin prickles with goosebumps.

The best way to warm up is body heat. I return the favor, raising Owen's sweater, teasing my fingers along his skin. He's gorgeous. Thick muscles to my leaner build, a shock of dark hair long enough for me to grab onto, and a mouth made for kissing mine. We're almost evenly matched in height, and that makes kissing even easier.

I lift off the sweater and then the long-sleeved tee that clings to him like a second skin. Holding his gaze, I slide the leather belt free of the buckle, then undo his button. The bulge in his jeans makes sliding his zipper down difficult, but I succeed and his light blue boxers poke through.

His hands close over my shoulders and his intake of breath drives my need higher. I push down his jeans, dragging the material until he can step out of them. The boxers are a slower journey. Thumbs hooked in the elastic, I take my time, pausing once his cock head is free to lick the tip.

"Greer." A plea in his tone, Owen slides one hand into my hair and the other to his boxers, pushing them down.

Not wanting to make him wait any longer, I shove the soft cotton out of my way. His erection springs free, thick and hard, and I wrap my hand around him even as he urges my head closer.

His scent is intensified here, mildly sweet and uniquely Owen. I draw the head into my mouth, run my tongue over the skin, poking into the slit. Sliding one hand along his shaft, I stroke the other over the tensing muscles in his thigh.

He splays his legs wider. "Damn, your mouth feels so good. I like you there. Sucking me. Tell me you like it."

I pull off of him with a pop. "I like it."

The hand fisting my hair relaxes and shifts into a caress. "Can you take me deeper?"

"Didn't I last time?" Without waiting for a response, I lean in and lick him from root to tip. My cock is aching for some attention, but I ignore it and concentrate on Owen.

Cradling his balls and stroking his length, I suck the head of his cock, and only begin taking him deeper when the hand in my hair glides to the back of my head and urges me down.

Loving the noises he makes, I take him until he hits the back of my throat. The long moan vibrating from his chest, the way his hand tightens in my strands again, and the broken whisper that is my name all spur me on. With lips and tongue and fingers, I draw more and more sounds from him.

The hand in my hair gently pulls and Owen's other hand trails over my temple. "Stop. I'm too close."

I can't resist another little suck, but I release my hold and allow him to draw free. He grabs my arms and hauls me to standing. His cock is pointing straight out and his pupils are blown.

His lips descend on mine. If they were hungry before, they are insatiable now, taking kiss after kiss. His hands land on my jeans and we both work to get the stiff fabric opened and off of me. My shorts quickly follow.

Hands on my shoulders, he back-walks me once more. In my long and narrow studio, there's only one destination—the bed along the back wall.

When we arrive, he spins me to face it, then draws me against his chest. Embracing me from behind, he glides his hands along my torso in strong, possessive strokes. "Tonight, at the party, when everyone was gathered in the room with the piano and you were singing and all eyes on you, do you know what I thought about?"

The touches are sizzling my nerve endings. "What?"

"Watching you on the field this season and knowing what you looked like under that uniform..."

I'm rock hard now, and aching for him to touch my dick. But he's keeping his hands everywhere else. Along my arms. Over my neck. Teasing my chest, stroking my sides.

His lips trail along the side of my neck. "Knowing how you like to be kissed..."

Muscles weakened, I angle my head to give him better access. He discovered that sensitive spot the first time we had sex, and he's exploited it every time. The way he kisses me there, I could melt into a puddle from that alone.

His hands move down my stomach and roam lower. And finally, they fist my cock. So hot, so good, I push into his tight grasp. "Knowing the sounds and expressions you make when you come... I'm the only one who knows these things."

Moaning and cock throbbing, I clench my hands at Owen's waist, turned on more by his words than any actual touching. He's never said things like this before, and he's never kissed me this much either.

"Owen." His name from my lips is a sigh.

"Get on the bed." He nudges me forward. I sink onto the bedspread on my hands and knees. Rummaging in the top drawer of the desk beside the bed, he grabs lube and a condom. He's watched me get them the other times and I guess he paid attention.

He settles behind me, kissing the back of my shoulder and smearing cool lube at my hole. As he opens me up, the kisses continue across the back of my neck before returning to that sensitive spot on the side.

My fingers tremble opening the condom for him. Fisting the bedspread, I drop onto my forearms, my pulse ticking in anticipation.

The slow push inside, he pauses to allow me to get used to him and waits for my okay before advancing further. When he's finally seated, I'm so full and more than ready for him to move.

The first thrusts are slow, sensual torture. One hand on my hip, Owen reaches for my cock, battling my hand away. "Let me stroke you."

His touch drives me too high, too fast. Grasping the spread and biting my lip, I fight the need thrumming through my body to come, seeking out every bit of pleasure.

The hand on my cock tightens and speeds up. I throw my head back, leaning into Owen's shoulder. "Fuck. Oh, fuck. Owen…"

His breath is unsteady, the thrusts of his hips increasing, harder and faster. "I'm right there too. Come for me so I can come in you."

Arching my back, I push my ass to meet his next push, and damn, the angle changes and his cock slides deeper. Owen shifts the hand from my hip to press against my prostate from the outside, the other hand works my cock like getting me to come first will let him win some competition.

His lips graze the side of my neck, teasing, then sucking hard. Groaning my pleasure, I'm on the verge of losing control. And he whispers, "Damn, I can't hold back. Come for me. Now."

The hint of the desperate desire in his voice, the press of his fingers on my skin, and I'm gone. Spiraling into pleasure, coaxed higher and higher by his pumping hips and clever hands.

Heartbeat pounding, I collapse onto my forearms. Owen's hands latch onto my hips. His groans and muttered curses fill the air. His hips shove forward, wild and pulsing, until finally he presses deep into me and stills, his fingers digging into my skin.

He falls on top of me, breathing ragged and presses a kiss to my cheek. We lay together as our heartbeats even out and our breathing returns to normal. I'm floating on a cloud of endorphins.

Drawing in his scent, I stroke my hand along his forearm, matching my breaths to his. He feels so good on top of me, like a weighted blanket of welcoming heat, sexy muscles, and banked strength.

He pushes onto his forearms and smiles down at me when I look back at him over my shoulder. "Consider that I.O.U. paid in full."

"I'm feeling pretty full right now." I squeeze my ass muscles around his cock.

Chuckling, he shifts back and securing the condom, pulls out of me. Immediately, the loss of his heat chills me. I lift off the bed enough to shove the quilt down so I can slide beneath its warmth.

"Be right back." He makes his way to the bathroom. Light from that open door spills into the room. Pipes squeak with the running water, then he returns carrying a wet washcloth which he tosses to me. It's warm, a thoughtful gesture, and one he never fails to deliver.

"Thanks." I wipe the cloth over myself and when I've finished, he tosses it into my clothes hamper.

Snuggled under the blanket, I watch him cover his sexy body with boxers, then jeans and socks. I want to reach for him, to cuddle with him, to ask him to stay, but we've never done that. We've agreed we're just having fun. Maybe he considers us to be friends too. Friends can share meals.

I take a breath and will my tense shoulders to relax and my suddenly pounding heart to stop beating like a wild thing caged in my chest. "You hungry? Want to order something? I was thinking of getting pizza or something from the late-night bakery."

Owen pulls on his T-shirt, then his sweater. "I better get going. I need to dictate some progress notes for patient charts tonight and I have an early start tomorrow."

"Okay." Smiling to cover the disappointment sinking my gut, I get up and pull on a pair of sweats from the pile of clean laundry on the chair.

"Hey, I didn't know you liked hockey too." Owen nods at the illustration of Striker, the furry, yellow, monster-like mascot of the Philadelphia Power, adorning my left pant leg.

"I haven't watched a game, so I don't know if I like it or not, but I think their mascot is awesome. Aspen got these for me after we saw Striker at the Pride parade in June, waving a flag with the Power's logo in the colors of the Pride and trans flags and hugging and high-fiving everyone."

He nods. "The Power organization does a lot for supporting the queer community in Philly. My practice became affiliated with the team this season, working with the players who are rehabbing from injuries."

I tug on the sweater I wore earlier tonight. "If you ever end up rehabbing Striker, will you get an autograph for me?"

Smiling, he smooths the material over my torso in what almost seems like an absent gesture. "Instead of wanting one of the players, like the leading scorer in the league or the guys who have won championships and awards, you want the mascot?"

I shrug like the touch isn't twisting my heart like a wet rag and then grin at Owen pressing the button to click on the shirt lights. "He's the only one I'd recognize..."

His laughter follows me as I lead him through the living room area.

Beside the tree, he stops to inspect the glass ball made to resemble a snow globe with Striker inside, wearing a Santa hat. "I didn't see the Striker ornament earlier. That's a great one."

"Kade and Easton gave it to me when they came over with Aspen and Apollo last week." The tradition of all of us buying our trees together and then helping decorate them are some of the things I look forward to most during the holidays.

Owen slips on his coat and shoes. The sound of the zipper rising precedes the click of the deadbolt and the twisting of the door handle. "I'll see you."

"Yeah." But I wonder when. All of our hookups have followed being brought together in some way with our teammates, and the spring rugby season doesn't start until the beginning of April. That's three and a half months away. But maybe this is for the best. Catching actual feelings for Owen isn't a wise thing at all. This gives me time for them to fade or work their way out of my system.

Making sure my features are placid, I open the door wider. "Drive safe."

He pauses beside me. Brown eyes, deep and intense, hold my gaze before dropping to my mouth. He leans in and his lips settle over my mouth. An electrifying charge zinging up my spine, I kiss him back, soaking up the warmth that is both firm and soft, and chasing his lips as they retreat. All too soon, my lips are bare and the air in front of me is cool and empty.

"Good luck with finals week." Palming his keys, Owen steps onto the small landing. "Don't work so hard you put off sleeping."

Nodding, I lift my hand in a wave then force myself to close the door so I don't watch him walk away like an infatuated fool.

Safely inside and alone, I touch my fingers to my buzzing lips. The goodbye kiss is new. He's never done that before. I don't know what to think of it, what it might mean—if anything—or what to think now at all. I have a long history of getting my romantic hopes up only to have them dashed. Hence, the mindset to stop looking so hard for love and just have fun while waiting for it to find me.

I don't know where Owen and I will or should go from here. If I can't shake these feelings for him, I should probably put a stop to our intermittent hookups the next time I see him. But if he starts seeing someone between now and then, I guess our time together would come to an end anyway.

The thoughts leave me colder than the chilly night air seeping past the frames of my apartment windows. I push away from the door and check to make sure each of the heavy curtains is smoothed and pulled shut to keep out the draft.

My gaze tracks to where Owen kissed me by the couch, and where he pulled off my sweater by the bed, and the mattress and how good he looked laying beside me. I'm not ready to give up the stolen moments with him. I'll just have to figure out a way to continue having them and not let my heart or feelings get in my way.

Swoon

♥

Firefighter Gage Garrison prides himself on being strong and reliable. Since his last relationship's humiliating end, he's kept to himself, but thanks to the rec league rugby club he joined, he's slowly gained new friendships and a place to belong. A place that is threatened when his attempts to rescue a kitten in a tree thrusts his secret fear of heights into the spotlight, in full view of his new friends, and the teammate he's been crushing on all season.

Dendrologist Valentine Bartley loves plants and trees with a passion. Settled in a new city, a new house, and a new job, he's now part of the rugby club he used to love playing against, and has formed some solid friendships there. He's also developed a crush on his fearless teammate Gage. Taking part in the tree rescue gives him a glimpse behind the tough mask Gage shows the world and he's determined, quirks and all, to pursue the intriguing man.

Caring for the kitten bonds the men. Sharing vulnerabilities and wants, they find support, honesty, and a connection that feels like the solid foundation for a relationship. But with Gage's worries over how his phobia could color Valentine's and his teammates' opinion of him, and Valentine's doubts over whether he can trust Gage to keep his word when others haven't, will fears of history repeating itself keep them from the promise of new beginnings they've found in each other?

Chapter One

Gage

Ominous gray clouds roll across the sky and the threat of coming rain perfumes the air brushing my forearms, face, and legs. Beneath the canopy of trees, I abandon the wide gravel trail in favor of more secluded, steeper grades and rugged paths carved by countless people over countless years. Perhaps coming here this afternoon wasn't wise, but the need to be surrounded by calming nature after four days of putting out fires was too big to ignore.

And since the forecasted thunderstorms have canceled rugby practice and my chance to see Valentine Bartley, being in my favorite place is also soothing my disappointment over not getting to spend time with my sexy ginger teammate.

Large boulders and smaller rocks shimmering with flecks of mica and garnet, twisted, gnarled tree roots and sky-skimming branches, the calming waters of Wissahickon Creek, the thick tree cover, in these dozens of miles of trails, I can forget that I'm in the heart of Philadelphia and its neighborhoods and people, and the busy rush of life in the city.

Faint mewing pulls me to a stop. Ears pricked, I attempt to gauge the direction and source. The wind carries the sound to me again. I turn, backtrack, the sound grows louder.

Muscles tense, I scan the dirt path, the plants, the larger rocks, and the fallen trees.

The mewing increases.

Above me.

High in the branches of an evergreen tree, a tiny black kitten perches on one of the upper branches. Its gold eyes meet my gaze. Glad this encounter isn't with one of the park's wild animals, I rest my foot on the base of the trunk. "How'd you get all the way up there?"

The mew is forlorn and the kitten looks scared, its tail straight up.

"Can you get down?" Keeping my voice soothing and soft, I extend my arm overhead. Several feet, more than double the length of my six foot three inch frame, separate us.

This kitten looks pretty young. I don't see a sign of its mother or siblings or a collar. I hope someone didn't dump it here.

I can't walk away. I don't know how long it's been up there or when it last had food or water or if it's injured and unable to get down. "Contrary to popular belief, having a fire department rescue you isn't an option. We generally don't respond to animal calls because we need to be available to help human emergencies. But I'll try to help you."

Climbing onto a broken, hollow log resting between the pine and another type of tree I can't name, I hope I'll only have to go up a few feet and can have the kitten comfortable enough to come to me. The weakened wood creaks and dips under my weight, but gets me high enough to use the other tree's wider, thicker branches to support my ascent. Branches and pine needles scraping my arms and legs, I heave myself higher and higher. The cat watches me, its tail lowering. I glance down to locate a new foothold, and the ground seems much farther away. My stomach clutches, my palms grow sweaty, and I fight the roll of fear.

Sucking in a breath, a step up another branch. "Once we get down, I can get you some food and water."

Raindrops fall, dotting my skin and clothes. The storm I was hoping would hold off until I got back to my car is apparently here.

"Great." My hands tighten around the rough branches. "Cats don't like water, right? Come with me. My truck is nice and dry."

Bargaining with a cat is something I did not envision occurring today. Or any day.

The splotches of water fall faster. With a crack followed by a thump, something below me falls. I tense, skin biting into the tree. The mewing kitten scurries up to a higher branch then presses against the trunk, its cry tugs at my heart. Golden eyes seem to be pleading with me.

Limbs shaking, using both trees, I climb up another few feet, breathing in the pungent scents of pine and wet leaves. If I were to stretch my arm overhead, I'd be able to brush my fingertips over the kitten's paw, but I doubt the branches above me will support my weight. "Please, just come down a little bit. I'll carry you the rest of the way. I understand being scared. I don't like heights either."

The kitten cocks its head, studying me. I dip my head to rub sweat and rain onto my shoulder and spy the ground so far below me, it seems like a mile away. My limbs freeze, my heart pounds, and icy terror strikes me.

I can't move. Not down. Not up. Not anywhere.

A roll of thunder rumbles in the distance like a sleeping giant on the verges of awakening. I don't know what to do.

The thunderstorms will be here soon, and the last place I want to be is in a tree. Adrenaline shoots through my muscles, but fear has me immobilized.

My phone pings from the pocket of my shorts. Being seen like this will be humiliating, but calling for help is my only option since my body refuses to cooperate. At least that will get the kitten to safety. I shift one hand along the branch in incremental centimeters until I reach the trunk, and continue the slow slide until I am hugging it tight.

With a shaky hand, I release my hold of the other branch so I can extricate my phone. The message notification is from our rugby club's group chat. I manage to thumb it open and tap the microphone to utilize the talk to text feature.

"Guys, I'm stuck in a tree in Wissahickon Valley Park. On a trail off of Forbidden Drive. I need help."

The message populates the chat, then I view the one above it, from Cam, my team's captain, reminding everyone that practice has been canceled due to the impending thunderstorms and a soggy field.

Message dots appear below my text.

Cam: Gage, you're seriously stuck in a tree?

Hugging said tree, I thumb the microphone icon again. "Yes, rescuing a cat. Now, we're both stuck. Dude, it's raining. I can't get down."

My message appears, then more message dots. Our teammate, and my closest friend in the club, Mateo chimes in.

Mateo: I have a ladder on my truck. Is the trail the one you and I walked on before?

Gratitude and the hope of rescue is swift and sweet, I hit the icon again. "Yes. I'm in the first trail on the right that shoots off the main one."

Mateo's response is right behind mine.

Mateo: Got it. Hang tight, bud. On my way.

Cam: I'll come too. Anyone free should come in case we need more bodies or more ladders. How tall is this tree?

"Ugh, I don't know. Really tall. I think I'm at least twenty feet up."

Another text immediately pops up.

Valentine: That park has a lot of oak, tulip, beech, and evergreen trees. Some of the trees top over one hundred feet. I'm coming too. Meet you all there.

Oh no. Not Valentine. The sexy ginger enchanted me from the first moment I saw him at a rugby practice at the end of March, and in the several weeks since, that interest has only grown. He's sweet and smart and has a great sense of humor. A dull throb beating in my temples, I clutch the tree, the bark biting my cheek, and I cringe because I don't want him to see me like this. I have to get down.

My gaze falls to the ground. My stomach drops and my limbs stiffen like an electric current is running through them. I can't move. I hate that I'm this way.

I'm thirty-one years old. A freaking firefighter. A gym rat. Six-foot-three and over two hundred pounds. At first glance, I look like I should be fearless. And yet, actually shifting my way down this tree seems impossible. Hell, even going down a fire pole still is enough to make my blood run cold, but if we are actually on our way to a fire or rescue, then something within overrides that fear. Squeezing my eyes shut, I try to channel whatever that is, but it refuses to surface.

With another tap on the group chat, I switch the setting so that any new messages will be read out to me, then slide the raindrop-dotted phone along my shirt as I transfer it back into my pocket.

The kitten and I stare at each other. Hugging the tree, I blink more water out of my eyes. Messages continue to roll in with teammates saying they're on their way. One comment on the irony of a fireman being stuck in a tree while rescuing a cat earns a bitter snicker.

I've managed to hide this fear from my coworkers and from pretty much everyone else who is a current part of my life. Not that there have been many people outside of work and the rugby team, not with my shift work and schedule.

Holding tight to the branches, I slide my sneaker an inch before the possibility of losing my footing and plunging to the ground freezes me in place. Keeping my ears pricked for sounds of anyone approaching, I wish I knew how many minutes have passed. "When my friends arrive, we'll get you down. You coming closer would help. Please?"

The *mew* and the zero movement from the furball is an apparent *no*.

Finally, my phone buzzes and the chat assistant's voice reads out the texts that my friends have arrived. I twist my head in the direction of the main trail. Faint laughter and conversations grow louder and closer. Then they come into view.

"There he is!" Cam calls out as he, Mateo, Valentine, and several other members of our club clamber down the path and gather by the base of the trees.

Mateo pushes the broken pieces of the log aside and rests an extendable ladder against the trunk of the wider tree. "This is the longest one I have. You okay, Gage?"

The metal edge of the ladder hits about a yard away from my sneaker.

"I..." My palms are sweaty, the dropping feeling in my stomach is back. "I... I'm stuck."

Cupping his hands around his mouth, Cam calls, "Your clothes are stuck?"

Before I can answer, Valentine studies me from where he's holding the ladder in place. "I'm coming up."

He shifts the ladder to the opposite side of the tree and with Mateo securing the hold, begins ascending. Alternating waves of embarrassment and fear of falling wash over me.

"Hey." A little breathless, he climbs the branches above the ladder with ease. Smile as warm as the shades in his light brown eyes, he comes to a stop on the other side of the trunk, almost level with me. In place of the contacts he wears for games and practices, dark brown glasses frame his eyes.

Concentrating on his freckles and smile, and that the rain has darkened his copper hair to russet, and how cute he looks in those glasses gives me a few seconds distraction from my predicament. "Hi. Uh, the kitten won't come down. I couldn't go any higher…"

"No worries, I'll go." Giving me glimpses of long, pale, freckled limbs and lithe muscles, he hauls himself higher then softens his voice and croons to the cat. "Come here, little one. An eastern white pine is no place for you. And straddling a pine and an oak is no place for Gage."

Of course, he'd know what type of trees these are. One of our teammates calls Valentine a tree doctor, but he's actually a dendrologist, which I've learned is someone who studies trees and woody plants.

Apparently, he's a cat whisperer too, because that little black fluff ball lets him lift it into his arm. Valentine tucks the kitten inside his partially unzipped hoodie.

"Let's get down." He makes his way back to being eye-to-eye with me, but one of the branches captures his hood, yanking him to a stop. The kitten mews and Val winces as though its claws have bitten through the material of whatever shirt he's wearing under that hoodie. "Damn. Can you reach over? I can't with the cat, too awkward an angle."

He bats one arm behind him as he talks, and my stomach lurches with worry that he'll fall. Reaching over means letting go. I shift my arm a centimeter and unease slithers up my spine. "I can't."

"Is your shirt or shorts caught on something? I can't see your one side from here. Maybe I can help you first." His gaze scans my body. When that gorgeous brown settles on my face, his expression shifts to concern, brows drawing together and forehead creasing.

I can assume he's guessed the real reason why I am stuck in this tree. Heat floods through me. My ears ring, drowning out calls and conversation from the guys down below.

Holding onto the trunk, Valentine lays his other hand over mine. "I'm here, I've got you. If I hold on to secure you, can you then reach over and tug my hood off the branch?"

I need to find bravery and try once again to pretend this is a rescue mission, even if all I am rescuing is an attempt to salvage my pride. "I can try."

With a brush along my knuckles, Val shifts his hand from mine and presses the firm digits against my shoulder. "I promise, Gage, I won't let you fall. You can do this."

My heart pounding, I loosen one shaky hand and clamp it on his shoulder and then force my fingers along the line of fabric up to the hood, and yank. Thankfully, the blue cotton comes free of the needled branch.

Val's hand is steady pressure on my shoulder until I return my hold to a branch. "You did good. Are you okay?"

Even though I'm not, I nod. "Sure."

The confident gaze behind rain-studded glasses holds me captive. "I'm going to help you down. We'll go together."

"Is the kitten okay?" My voice as rough as the tree's bark, I glance at the bundle moving inside his hoodie.

"Clinging to my shirt, but fine." Val lays his hand atop mine once more. He opens his mouth like he's about to say something else, then pauses, closes it. Leaving me desperate to know whatever he is choosing to hold back, he taps my hand. "Move this first to the branch right below. I'll shift down a bit and tap your leg and guide it to the next branch. Keep your eyes on me if you want."

Releasing my hold of the one branch is okay. Letting go of the hug I've had on the trunk for close to an hour is a lot harder. The tap to my leg is accompanied by his hand sliding up my calf as I lower myself. Heart hammering, stomach in my throat, I find the next foothold.

"Good job, Gage. You're doing great." Val's quiet encouragement continues, and he again taps my leg. "Next one is a little to your left. That's it."

Staying about a foot ahead of me, he keeps touching my back, hip, and legs, lending security to my movements.

With Cam, Mateo, and the others cheering us on, we reach the ladder. He helps me get my feet onto the metal rungs, then with a hand on my back, supports me until I can shift down to get my hands on it too. Switching to the ladder is easier to judge where the next foothold will be, and the familiarity of use takes over. Even so, Val stays with me, matching his descent to mine.

Teo steps away from where he'd been securing the ladder, and I clear the last five rungs with ease. Back on solid ground, limbs trembling, I stumble into Cam and he bearhugs me. Nearly as big as I am, his solid build is a welcome support.

Clapping my back, he pulls away. "Dude. This was like a team building activity. I'm glad you're down now. The storms they're calling for tonight look like they'll be pretty severe."

"Thanks for coming." Aware of Valentine reaching the ground, I turn from Cam to Mateo. "Thanks for bringing the ladder."

Gaze zeroing in on my face, he clasps hold of my shoulder. "I'm just glad I still had it on my truck. You okay?"

"Sure. Great. Yeah. Thanks again." Teo's pretty perceptive, and I hate that he might think less of me now. I let my attention get caught by teammates Owen, Apollo, and our manager, Hercules, and exchange quick back slaps with them and then nod at Aspen, Greer, Easton, and Kade who play for the club's under-thirty team.

Unease rips through me like a flash flood. They all witnessed my near-paralyzing fear. How can they trust me to be a fearless player on the pitch now, with the game against our biggest rival coming up in three days and the need of a win to make the playoffs? I'm expecting the ridiculing to begin any second.

Valentine approaches, cuddling the still-bundled kitten against his chest. His teeth sink into his lower lips and his eyes seem a bit too bright. "Hey, I wanted to ask... Do you..."

Red alerts fire in my brain that Valentine is about to ask if I have acrophobia or if I've considered seeking treatment for my fear of heights.

Fishing for my keys, I back up a step. "I'm sorry. I have to go. Thanks for coming, guys. I owe you all one."

Lightning cracks across the sky, followed by booming thunder. The rain falls faster, heavier.

"We'd better take cover." Grateful for the excuse the weather is providing, I rush down the muddy trail, muscles burning to ensure I have a good lead over the others.

There's no way I can return to playing rugby with these guys. Valentine knows for sure about my phobia. The others are probably aware from watching my guided, shaky descent, and if not, they will be once he shares how panicked I was in that tree. And that sucks. I'd thought I'd found something special with this group of guys when I joined the club last season. And now, I'm afraid that's gone. It's going to be like the ramifications from my buddy's bachelor weekend all over again, when my fear was front and center and I became a joke and a punchline.

My chance with Valentine is gone too. What guy is going to want someone they had to rescue from a fear inside their head?

Find these books and more at:
   https://www.shelleyandmer.com/books

Our VIP reader newsletter is the *best* way to stay in the know about our new releases, projects, and other special events.

Sign up at:
https://www.shelleyandmer.com/newsletter

Also By Susan & Chantal

Love & Rugby

Spiral

Spark

Smolder

Shine

Surprise

Swoon

Love & Rugby: Season of Love

Savor

Seduce

Stay

Philadelphia Power

Against the Rush

Over the Top (Coming Soon)

Also By Susan

Philadelphia Frenzy
Mad Scramble

Buffalo Bedlam
Skating on Chance
Holding on Tight
Scoring Slater

Bliss Bakery
Sugar Crush

Falling series
Falling Faster

For Susan's full book list, please go to:
https://www.susanscottshelley.com/books

Also By Chantal

Absolving Ash

Love in Philly
Where I Belong

For Chantal's full book list, please go to:
https://www.chantalmer.com/books-1

About Susan

USA TODAY bestselling author Susan Scott Shelley writes romances with heat and heart that celebrate love without limits. Enormous mugs of coffee and tea make her happy, as does reading romance novels and binging episodes of her favorite British TV shows. Susan also works as a professional voiceover artist, and while she's definitely a city girl, she likes being out in nature as often as possible. A fan of mythology, word games, and hockey, she lives in Philadelphia with her husband and has yet to meet a plant she hasn't wanted to take home.

Visit her website for her full book list, excerpts, and more:
http://www.susanscottshelley.com

About Chantal

Chantal Mer never set out to write books. Yet here she is, and she's having a blast. Happily ever afters for everyone makes her heart sing. When she's not writing, Chantal can be found walking her adorable dog, going to musical theater with her daughter, observing the night sky with her husband and his telescope, and learning about the latest advances in video games with her son. Give her a book and a glass of wine and she's in her happy place. Chantal lives outside of Philadelphia with her husband, two teens, her sweet pup, Miss Toffee, and her big orang tabby cat, Simba.

To keep up to date with Chantal, check out her website. https://chantalmer.com/

Sign up for Chantal's reader newsletter: https://chantalmer.com/newsletters/